The Dadhunters

To Ruairi and Mari Frances,
my little helpers

The Dadhunters

JOSEPHINE FEENEY

Collins

An imprint of HarperCollinsPublishers

First published in Great Britain by Collins in 1996

3 5 7 9 10 8 6 4

Collins is an imprint of HarperCollins*Publishers* Ltd,
77-85 Fulham Palace Road, Hammersmith,
London W6 8JB

The HarperCollins website address is
www.fireandwater.com

ISBN 0 00 185653-7
ISBN 0 00 675178-4

Printed and bound in Great Britain by
Caledonian International Book Manufacturing Ltd,
Glasgow G64

ONE

Gary NcNab, conqueror of the Brecon Beacons, rubbed his eyes in disbelief as the coach pulled into the school drive. There, side by side, stood his mum and dad, waiting for his homecoming. The way they were standing it almost looked as though they were back together again. On the journey home he'd felt sad that a brilliant camping holiday had ended and he wasn't looking forward to coming home to just him and his mum about the house. But now this!

"Welcome home, son!" Gary's dad said, ruffling his hair as he stepped off the coach. He was still wearing his smart work suit.

"Look at the state of you!" his mum said as she hugged him, smiling and laughing. "What have you been up to?"

"Abseiling, pony trekking, canoeing, hill walking – it was brilliant, pure brilliant, Mum!"

"And I suppose this bag is filled with mud-encrusted clothes – a souvenir of the Brecon Beacons, eh Gary?" his mother jested. "Phew!" she said, pinching her nose comically as she looked inside. She didn't seem in the least bit annoyed that his bag actually was full of filthy washing.

"You've caught a bit of a tan as well, son," his dad remarked as they walked over to thank the teachers.

"You're joking aren't you?" Mum said. "That's ingrained dirt from a week free of washing his face!"

"I did wash, Mum, honest. It was just that—" Gary tried to explain.

"It doesn't matter, love. I'm only joking. It does you good to get away from your mother's nagging for a week, doesn't it?"

"Yes," Gary laughed too. He looked around to see the playground was buzzing with reunited families, stories spilling out about the state of tents and the canoeing expeditions. Gary smiled as he saw Robert, his best friend, wriggle off his mother's hug. Mr Doyle, his class teacher, was breathing a huge sigh of relief as parents shook his hand and thanked him for taking such good care of their precious offspring. Gary felt good to be back.

They all drove home in Dad's car. Gary

hadn't been in the car with his mum and dad since his father had left nearly eighteen months ago. Now, Gary only saw his dad on his own every other Saturday. Dad was silent as Gary's mum asked a hundred questions about the adventure holiday.

"What was the food like?"

"Not bad," Gary replied.

"Do you mean it was better than my cooking?"

"Um . . ." Gary hesitated.

"You don't have to answer that, Gary. Were you able to sleep at night?"

"A bit."

"Did you clean your teeth? Did you behave? Was it great fun?"

"Yes, yes, yes," Gary sighed. "I like your new car, Dad."

"Thanks, son. One of the few perks," Dad said, quietly.

"Never mind the car, Gary! Tell us about the holiday!" Gary's mum and dad laughed together at her impatience.

Back home, Dad parked the car and slowly followed Gary and his mum into the house.

"Now then – get up those stairs and have a good bath. There's lots of hot water. Don't forget to scrub behind your ears. I've left some clean clothes on your bed," Mum said as soon as they walked into the house. "I'll sort out this bag and then —"

"Are you staying, Dad?" Gary asked hopefully from halfway up the stairs. His dad seemed to be taking ages to wipe his feet, almost as though he was frightened to walk too far into the house.

"We're all going out for a meal together, Gary," his mother said quickly before Dad had a chance to reply. "You choose – say where you want to go."

"Really?" Gary asked. "This is pure, dead brilliant Mum!" It was.

"Now, go on. Get up those stairs and get scrubbing. I bet there's spuds and carrots growing behind your ears," Mum said, laughing.

Gary raced up the rest of the stairs. A few minutes later he jumped into his Supersonic Outer Space bath foam and started to scrub the Brecon Beacons from his legs and arms. Only they weren't his legs and arms any more. They were the million pound limbs of Tyrone Bradley, City's brand new signing and Gary's complete hero.

"This is great," he said to himself. "One more match and we'll win the Premiership! Yesss!" Gary fired the soap into the bath, emptying half of the foam in the process. The water was getting cold.

"Do I have to wash my hair?" Gary shouted. "Only I washed it last Monday before we went."

"Course you do," his mum said, appearing suddenly at the bathroom door. "Now get a move on, Gary. Where would you like to eat?"

Eugene McNab was able to park his new car right outside Gino's House. It was really called *La Casa Gino* but Gary thought it was silly having an Italian name for a restaurant when it was in England. Anyway, this was where he wanted to eat. He loved their spaghetti bolognese, oozing with tomato sauce, and the garlic bread. Ooh – and the Italian ice-cream. Gary didn't even look at the menu – he knew exactly what he wanted.

"Why don't you try something different this evening, son? Now that you've been away from home for the first time," Dad suggested while perusing the menu. Gary's dad was like that – always encouraging him to try new things.

Gary knew the proper way to eat spaghetti. Ages ago, his dad had taught him how to wrap the pasta carefully around his fork, scooping up some of the delicious sauce at the same time. That's why he always chose spaghetti – it was hard to eat but he knew how. Unlike some of his friends at school who chopped it up, making it look like baby food.

The waiter placed a glass of coke in front of Gary and asked, "The usual?"

Gary laughed. "Yes please."

"Where you lot been then? Ain't seen you for ages. Must be about a year," the waiter remarked in an Italian accent.

"Busy!" Dad said, placing both hands flat on the table. "Very busy, what with one thing and another." It had been over a year since they were last there. At the time, Gary's mum and dad had wanted to prove that they could still do things together, as a family, every so often. It had been a long time.

"So . . . tell us about the camping holiday," Dad said brightly when their order had been taken.

"Oh, Dad, it was just brilliant! We slept in big green tents, on like . . . camp beds. Every morning we had to make our own sandwiches before we went off to our activity. We did all sorts – you know, canoeing, sailing, raft building — " Gary's mum and dad listened attentively.

"Garlic bread," the waiter announced, placing the food on the table with a flourish.

Gary snatched hungrily at a large triangular piece. "I've been dreaming about this," Gary said. They all laughed.

"Anyways, Dad," Gary said, his mouth full of food. "What are you doing here? What's happened this week – while I've been away?" His voice was full of hope and expectation.

"Ah, yes," Dad said, clearing his throat. "Your mother and I have something to tell you—"

"No, Gary – your *dad* has something he wants to tell you," Bernadette McNab interrupted.

By the time the spaghetti arrived at the table, Gary had lost his appetite. He nodded quietly when the waiter asked if he wanted cheese and pepper atop his bolognese sauce. He didn't even feel like any Italian ice-cream. Not since he'd heard Dad's news.

TWO

They parked their bikes along the grassy bank at the side of the canal. "Let's see who can get a stone to leap over the weir," Gary suggested, laughing.

Robert started. He was brilliant at skimming stones, choosing only flat, slightly rounded specimens from the alleyway that led down to the canal. They didn't notice the Canada geese fluttering nervously and moving along closer to the gasworks as the stones flew over the weir.

"Hey, you lads!" a woman shouted. "What are you playing at? Can't you see you're frightening the birds? Now put those stones down and stop it!"

She watched as they emptied their pockets of the skimming stones. "We didn't mean to," Robert protested. "We were just having a game to see who could—"

"I'm sure!" the woman said. "You

youngsters, you're all alike – no respect for nature." Then, pulling her dog as if he'd been throwing stones too, she continued to walk along the tow path.

Gary and Robert fell on to the grassy bank next to their bikes. They could see her watching them from behind a bridge, further along the canal. They laughed and lay back, enjoying the early evening sun. "Weren't it brilliant last week?" Gary said.

"Yeah, best holiday ever. Can't wait to go back," Robert agreed.

"Me too. It was great when you fell off the pony," Gary said, giggling.

"I never fell off," Robert shouted, giving his friend a shove. "I just got off 'cos the saddle wasn't right."

"No you didn't!"

"Anyways, you were scared of that abseiling tower," Robert taunted.

"No I wasn't! That helmet hurt my ears."

"No it didn't. You were scared."

"But I did it in the end," Gary protested.

"Only after Doyle threatened you'd go home if you didn't."

"He did not! He said, 'If you can abseil down this tower, you can do anything.' So I did it."

"I'm glad we were in the same group," Robert said.

"And the same tent."

"Only because I told Mr Doyle I was frightened of the dark and I needed to be near my best friend!" Robert said, laughing.

"He's all right, Mr Doyle," Gary said.

"Yeah – he's sound!" Robert agreed.

Gary leaned forward. "Hey, guess what?" he said, prompting Robert to sit up. He'd been longing to tell Robert what his dad had told him at Gino's House. Robert spun his bike's back wheel as he listened.

"My dad's getting married again," he said. He wanted it to sound as though it wasn't important, as though it didn't matter all that much.

"Who to?" Robert asked, spinning the wheel slowly.

"His girlfriend, Karen. You know, the one who works in the shop." Gary's voice sounded like it belonged to someone else.

"When did you find out?" Robert asked, his bike wheel now still.

"On Friday, after the holiday."

They sat in silence, for what seemed like ages, digesting the news.

"Bet your mum'll get a boyfriend now," Robert said sagely.

"She won't."

"She will, Gary – they all do. My mum said

she wouldn't ever have any more boyfriends. She said she hated men. Then as soon as Dad had another kid, she started bringing Ronan home."

"What's it like having him there?" Gary asked.

"He's not too bad, actually. He's a long distance lorry driver. He's not at home much."

"I'd hate it if I had to have another dad," Gary said quietly, almost afraid to voice his fears. "Karen's bad enough."

"Do you know what I think, Gary?" Robert said, thoughtful for once. "I think it would be better if we chose the new boyfriends for our mums. It'd be much better."

"Yeah," Gary said, miles away.

"I mean, why can't my mum have a boyfriend who plays for City? She's always saying that footballers have got nice legs and I'd probably be able to get into matches for nothing. That'd be pure dead brilliant."

"Yeah," Gary said, suddenly more interested. He stared at the Canada geese sitting quietly along the top of the weir.

"And I'd probably get a new City strip every season – and mentioned in the club programme. And we'd probably be on the front page of the *Mercury* when they got married. Do you want to skim some more stones?" Robert asked.

"No. That woman's still up there spying on us and, anyways, I'd better get back. I'm not really allowed down by the canal. My mum would be furious if she knew."

To avoid punctures they wheeled their bikes quickly back up the alleyway next to the industrial estate. Then they cycled back along the busy streets.

"You're right Robert," Gary said wistfully. "It would be best if we chose for them."

"Why don't you?" Robert said, confidently.

"How could I?" said Gary.

"If we can abseil down a tower, we can do anything," Robert said.

"Remember that bit where you go over the edge? Weren't it awful that?" he added, shuddering at the memory.

"But weren't it brilliant when you get near the ground and you know you're safe," Gary said.

"Brilliant!" Robert said. "Bet it would be dead easy to find a man for your mum."

"Easier than learning how to trot on a pony!" Gary said. "Come on, let's get back!"

THREE

Gary closed his eyes and thought about the day he'd sat on his dad's shoulders when he was only six – the day City had won the league. He had felt so tall and happy he had imagined he'd be able to touch the Town Hall clock. He could almost feel his dad's hands gripping his ankles in their bright blue cartoon socks, making sure he wouldn't fall off cheering for the first goal.

Mum was always back home in those days. "We won!" Gary used to shout as he ran through the house after the match.

"I know. I heard on the radio."

"It was brill, Mum. I sat on Dad's shoulders," Gary would say as his mum and dad spun around the room, waltzing to a tune Dad whistled.

"I'm glad they won, pet," Mum said. "You see, I burnt the pie. I was writing an essay on multiple births – that's twins, before you ask,

Gary – and I lost track of the time!"

Dad laughed and hugged her. Gary wrapped his arms around the back of his mum. "We'll go to the chippy. Anyway, you weren't supposed to be cooking. Did you finish your essay?"

At that time, Bernadette was always writing essays. She was training to be a midwife and there was a lot of studying involved. Even when she wasn't writing essays, she wasn't much of a cook.

Gary used to love going to the supermarket with his mum. She'd pick really exciting new things from the freezers and say, "Shall we try this, Gary? It only takes five minutes to cook. More time for playing!"

Why didn't it stay like that? Not always sitting on Dad's shoulders but . . . Dad and him going to the football and coming home to burnt pies and waltzing and fish and chip suppers and Mum writing essays. Now, he only saw his dad every other Saturday when City were playing at home.

"When you're ready, Gary McNab," Mr Doyle said in a voice filled with impatience, "we'll continue . . . . Chapter Five: *The Secret Methods.*"

"You'll get done if you don't stop daydreaming," Robert whispered. "Mr Doyle said we'll be tested on these two chapters when he's finished reading."

It was easy for Robert – it was years and years since his mum and dad divorced. He didn't really know his dad all that well and he was used to his mum's boyfriend.

Gary hated Karen. When Dad had said he was going to live with her so that they could all be happy, he had hated his dad. "What about me, Dad?" Gary had asked. "Won't you miss me?"

"It's best for everyone," Dad had said. "Your mum has a busy career and I want to be with Karen." It hadn't made Gary happy. He felt very, very sad.

Everyone was crying that night – apart from Karen. She sat outside in a van, waiting to load up Dad's things, reading a glossy magazine. She was chewing gum and looking at her watch from time to time. Gary saw her through the net curtains when she thought nobody was looking. He wanted to slap her for taking his dad like he'd wanted to slap the boy who had taken Robert from him in infant school. But the next day Robert was his friend again.

"I'll always be your dad, son. I'll always be there for you whenever you need me. And, of course, we'll always go to see City together."

"Gary McNab!" Mr Doyle shouted. "What's the matter with you today? That's the second

21

question I've asked you. It seems as though you're inhabiting another universe."

"Sorry, Dad, I mean . . . I mean . . . . Sorry. Sorry, Sir!" Gary stammered. The class laughed raucously.

"That's enough! That's enough," Mr Doyle said in a softer tone, smiling. "We all make mistakes. Now calm down. Right then, Gary. I'll ask you again."

It was always hard at the end of the afternoon when Mr Doyle read them another episode from the story. He was brilliant at telling stories – just like Gary's dad. It always reminded Gary of the days he'd sat snuggled up close to his father and heard about wild cats, friendly monsters, kind postmen and naughty children.

"I'll always be your dad, son." Gary wasn't sure if he wanted him to be his dad anymore. Not if it meant that Karen was going to be his stepmother – his wicked stepmother.

Mr Doyle slammed the book shut, as he usually did, at a particularly dramatic point. "Right then, how will Danny's dad catch the pheasants?" he asked, scanning the class with his index finger. Hands shot up, pointing urgently at the ceiling. "Sir, Sir!" almost everyone cried.

"Gary," Mr Doyle said. He was always doing that – choosing the one person who didn't have their hand up.

"With sticky raisins," Gary said in an uninterested voice. It was a method that had kept poking through his afternoon thoughts. It couldn't be anything else. Mr Doyle looked surprised that Gary had provided the right answer.

"Well done. Not bad for someone who is only a temporary resident of this planet." The class laughed quietly, unsure about Mr Doyle's joke. "Right then, more of *Danny, the Champion of the World* tomorrow. Chairs up, line up!" It was the usual afternoon dismissal chant. As soon as the bell rang Mr Doyle would shout, "Afternoon all. Off you go and . . . be careful!" The class joined in with the last two words – like an audience on a game show.

"Gary," Mr Doyle said as the class trailed out. "Everything all right? Anything I need to know? You're not going to tell me you're unfit for the next match against—"

"No, Sir, I'm fine," Gary said, looking at Robert and grinning.

"He's got a lot on his mind," Robert said, wisely.

"Oh, yes? Lucky he's got you, Trouble, to help him," Mr Doyle said, easing himself into a comfortable leaning position against his untidy desk.

"I was thinking about my dad," Gary said,

still looking at Robert and trying not to giggle. He felt so daft telling a teacher about things at home. In a quiet moment, on the bus home from the adventure holiday, Gary had told Mr Doyle about his mum and dad and Karen. He didn't know the whole story though and Gary didn't want to tell him.

"Oh, I see. Was it something in the story?" Mr Doyle asked quietly. "Did something start you off, thinking about your dad?"

"Sort of . . . but I'm all right now," Gary said, briskly.

"Fine. Just so long as I know, son." Mr Doyle ruffled Gary's hair. That hurt. It was too much like Dad.

On the way home Gary tried to shrug it from his mind. He dribbled his yellow football along the narrow pavement, annoying the mums and dads who were collecting their little ones from the infant school. When the pavement was clear, Gary started to pick up speed, leaving Robert dawdling behind.

"And City's new signing, Tyrone Bradley, dribbles down the right wing and nudges the ball to McLean. Oh, what a wonderful pass!"

Robert ignored the ball. "Robert!" Gary shouted changing from his commentator's voice back to normal. "What you playing at? The other side could have scored by now."

"Remember what we were saying about your mum?" Robert said, thinking aloud. "Yesterday, remember?"

Gary gathered the ball up under his arm and headed the air as they walked along together. "I don't know if I want to do anything like that."

"Then your mum'll just marry someone awful," Robert reminded Gary. "But if *we* choose someone for your mum—"

"Like who?" Gary said.

"I don't know yet, but I've got an idea."

"Oh, yeah," said Gary suspiciously. He knew all about Robert's big ideas.

"We could draw up a list of suitable people, ones who like football and things like that," Robert suggested.

"Do you mean a shortlist, like they do for the England manager's job?"

"Yes," Robert agreed. "Something like that."

"All right then," Gary said. "Where shall we start?"

FOUR

They really hadn't a clue where to start.

Back at Robert's house, Gary and Robert discussed the plan. "Right then," Robert said, pen in hand over a blank piece of paper. "Who shall we put on the shortlist?"

Gary's mouth was too full of cake to answer. "And then what shall we do?" Gary asked when his mouth was eventually empty. "How could we get them together?"

"I don't know. I'm not sure," Robert said. "We need to do this shortlist first."

"Yes, I suppose so," Gary agreed. "We only want people who we think are all right. People who like football and telly and—"

"Now, what's this you're talking about?" Robert's gran asked. She cut another slice of the delicious lemon cake that she'd made especially for Robert. Robert's gran was looking after him while his mum and Ronan were in Spain.

Robert hurriedly covered the sheet of paper. For a moment he was stunned by his gran's question. Gary stared at Robert, waiting, too, for his reply. "We know this lady who's looking for a husband and we're trying to help her," Robert said. Gary smiled at this reply.

Robert's gran was highly amused. She laughed for ages and then burst into a fit of coughing. Gary and Robert couldn't see what was so funny. "You're like little matchmakers," she said, between giggles and coughs.

"Matchmakers?" Gary asked, puzzled. "How do you mean?"

"Now Gary," she said, brushing cake crumbs away from her place at the table and leaning forward, "where I came from in Ireland, there was no such thing as meeting people by chance and dating. My mother and father were brought together by a matchmaker."

"How do you mean?" Gary asked again, between mouthfuls of cake.

"Well, if you wanted to get married, your mother and father would go to the matchmaker in the village and say, 'Would you find somebody for my daughter or son.' They would arrange things with another family and so a couple would be brought together and eventually they'd marry."

"But what if they didn't like one another?" Gary asked.

"Well, funnily enough, in most matches I heard of, the pair grew to like one another. The matchmaker made sure the two young ones had something in common. Like Honoria Quinn and Tomas Hughes. She played the fiddle and he played the button accordion. They were a great match! And didn't the marriages last in those days? Sure, there was no such thing as divorce!"

Gary looked at the line of lemon cake crumbs pushed aside by Robert's granny. It would have been nice if his Mum and Dad had been brought together by a matchmaker. Dad might still be living at home.

"So, Robert, what are you doing with the pen and paper?" Robert's gran asked.

"We were going to make a shortlist."

"Arrah, Robert, you don't need that!"

"What shall we do then?" Gary asked.

"Well, I'll tell you now, lads. This is what you'll do if you want to help this lady. Watch her." Robert's gran's face was creased with concentration. She pointed to her eyes.

"What do you mean, Gran?" Robert asked.

"Watch her because I'll bet any money she already has her eye on someone if she's looking for a husband. Watch the way she talks to any of the young men she meets and if there's a little extra twinkle in the eye or a lot of laughter whenever she meets a certain person, well then – that's your man!"

Robert leaned forward. "What shall we do then, Gran, when we've found out who she likes?"

"Then you'll have to think of something – it won't be too much to give her just a little push in the right direction. You know what I mean, Gary, because I can see you smiling!" She gently nudged Gary's shoulder. He couldn't help thinking how easy it sounded.

Robert and Gary watched Bernadette very closely indeed over the next few days. She grew rather tired of their mooning about after her. "Is there something wrong with my face?" she asked.

It wasn't so easy because she smiled with an extra twinkle and laughed with almost everyone she met.

On Saturday morning, Gary and Robert accompanied her to the supermarket. "What about him?" Robert asked, nodding towards the cashier as they stood a little way beyond the checkout.

"He's about fifteen!" Gary said, dismissing Robert's suggestion. "You're not watching properly, Robert."

"What about him?" Robert asked a little later as they stood outside the local butchers.

"She's always like that when she wants an extra pork chop," Gary said. "This is rubbish, Robert."

Robert had to agree. Bernadette was so charming to almost everyone, that it was impossible to see if she especially liked someone.

By the following Monday morning, Robert and Gary had almost given up hope. Then Gary forgot his P.E. kit.

His mum noticed it later, slumped against the radiator in the hall. She decided to take it into school on her way to work.

Bernadette stopped Mr Doyle as his class were leaving assembly. "Mr Doyle!" she called.

"Hello, Mrs McNab. How nice to see you. Is there a problem?" They stood to one side of the main corridor.

"No." It was then that Robert noticed Bernadette smile sweetly at his teacher. He pulled Gary aside and they watched, half-hidden by a staircase.

"Gary!" Robert hissed. "Look at your mum."

Gary wasn't sure that Robert was on about. A long, boring assembly had meant that his mind had wandered back to the Brecon Beacons.

"Oh, no! What's up now?" he said, half to himself as he finally noticed his mum and Mr Doyle talking. They were laughing about something.

"No, I mean, look at the way your mum's talking," Robert said. "Remember what my gran said?"

Gary had forgotten.

"Do you want me to give it to him?" Mr Doyle asked.

"Oh no, it's all right. He's over there with Robert. Gary!" She waved to the two boys. Then she turned back to Mr Doyle and gently placed her hand on his arm. "Those two boys are inseparable – like Siamese twins." Then she leaned back and laughed.

So did Mr Doyle. "Trouble and Double," he said, pointing at Robert first and then Gary.

"Look at that!" Robert said.

"What? What you on about?"

"Your mum. That's it!" said Robert.

"That's what?" said Gary.

"Gary . . ." Robert looked serious. "I think she's madly in love with Mr Doyle!"

Gary's mouth fell open in amazement.

"Gary, come on," his mum called. He walked towards her as if she were an alien. "Aren't I good to you? Here's your P.E. kit. Now if you weren't in such a dream half the time you would have remembered it."

"Thanks, Mum" Gary muttered.

"Got a kiss for your mum?" she asked. Mr Doyle moved away towards his class, shouting at those who dawdled.

"Mum!" Gary squirmed. He knew from his mother's expression that she was only teasing. He ran off to rejoin his class.

Meanwhile, Robert had an idea, a very good idea. He couldn't wait to tell Gary his plan.

FIVE

"How about a Mediterranean pizza for tea?" Bernadette asked that evening.

"OK," Gary agreed. He was busy reading the match report all about the famous Tyrone Bradley's first appearance in a City strip. He hadn't played all that well. The million-pound limbs didn't seem to be working properly. The *Mercury* even suggested that City might have wasted their money.

"Mediterranean pizza should be swimming in blue seas and sunshine. But I suppose red peppers and stringy cheese will have to do. Is that all right for you, Gary?"

"OK," murmured Gary, his mind still on Tyrone.

"Would you mind coming down from Planet Walnut for a minute?"

Gary laughed. His mum was always saying that. Quite often he was miles away, thinking about . . . well, all sorts of important things.

Robert called for Gary after tea. "You won't go down near the canal, will you?" Gary's mum warned as the two boys wheeled their bicycles out of the garden.

Robert tugged at Gary's sleeve so that he wouldn't answer her question.

"Bye, Mum" Gary shouted.

"Are we still going to have a shortlist, like the England manager's job?" Gary asked as they cycled away.

"For your mum?" Robert said. Gary nodded silently in agreement. "I think your mum needs someone who can cook. That pizza looked disgusting."

"That's 'cause she didn't leave it in the oven for long enough," Gary said.

"Exactly!"

"Don't you think it would be better if we only had people who liked the same things as us?" Gary suggested.

"Do you mean like football and cricket and telly?"

"Yes. And someone who lets you stay up a bit later than most parents," Gary said.

They climbed on to the canal embankment, lifting their bikes carefully over the spiky fence. For a few moments they were silent as they negotiated their way down to a comfortable spot.

"But, what about Mr Doyle?" Robert said, breaking the silence. They were back next to the Canada geese, watching two barge people struggling with the lock.

"What about him?" Gary asked, skimming a stone over the still, pond-like canal. The Canada geese jumped slightly.

"For your mum? You saw the way they were talking to one another this morning. Remember what my gran said? I think they really like one another and he'd be brilliant! He gets loads of free tickets for City what with him being coach for our school team. And he's pally with Stephan Kanchinski, City's goalie."

"No," Gary said, half-heartedly.

"We'll have to think about how they can meet up," Robert said, not hearing Gary as his thoughts raced ahead. "Yes, he'd be brilliant. Your mum would like him too. My mum always says he's good looking. How about this?" Robert said, carried along with his scheme. "I've got a great idea, listen . . ." The Canada geese waded towards the two boys as if they were also involved in the plot.

It was a good idea. A very good idea.

SIX

"What have you been up to at school?" Bernadette asked, a week later.

"Nothing, Mum. Why?" Gary replied with mock innocence. He'd been rehearsing this scene for days.

"There's a letter in the post today from Mr Doyle. He says he needs to talk to me about your progress."

"I think it's a general letter for all parents" Gary replied, slowly chewing the last bit of toast.

"Perhaps it's best if we ring your dad and we can go up together, just in case there's any bother. He likes dealing with the teachers—"

"No, Mum," Gary pleaded.

Bernadette examined the note. The paper looked a bit scrunched and dog-eared. "He's not that good at spelling, your Mr Doyle. And he hasn't spaced his paragraphs out correctly.

36

That's a bit worrying."

"I'll have to tell him." Gary said, cheekily.

"Who? Mr Doyle? Don't be daft, Gary – and land yourself in more trouble."

"I'm not in trouble, Mum."

"Well, I don't care. I think your dad should be there too if Mr Doyle has something to say about your future. Look how he's spelt 'progress' – two 'r's and one 's'. I'll have to have a word with him about that," Mum said, thumping the letter.

"Oh, don't, Mum, you'll show me up." Gary cringed at the thought.

"And look how he's spelt 'meeting'." Bernadette waved the letter again. "M e a t i n g. Honestly, it doesn't exactly inspire confidence in your teachers, does it? Do you know what I can't understand, Gary? If people are so bad at typing, why don't they send a handwritten note?"

"When are you going to see him?" Gary asked. He felt really angry with Robert for making those stupid mistakes. It had been Robert's brilliant idea to forge a letter from Mr Doyle to his mum.

"Let's check the spellings," Gary had said before they printed the letter.

"No need," Robert had said, confidently. "There's a sort of automatic spell-check on my computer."

"Don't be daft, Robert. There's no such thing as an automatic spell-check."

"There is on mine," Robert assured Gary. "Now, stop worrying." Robert was the sort of boy who appeared to know everything and even if he didn't know some things he pretended he did. "This is a brilliant idea, Gary," Robert had said as they leaned over the computer, trying to write a letter in the sort of language used by teachers.

It would have a been a good idea – if only they'd got the spelling right.

Gary's mum checked her diary, flipping the pages over quickly. "I'm that busy. Why didn't he speak to me when I was in school the other day? How about next Tuesday after school? There's a meeting then but I'll rearrange."

"OK, Mum I'll tell Mr Doyle. Straight after school?" Gary said as he was about the leave the house.

"You'll do no such thing! I'll write him a quick note."

It was a lovely April morning and as Gary walked to school he felt quite happy. He was thinking about who'd be in his team in today's playground match. Then Robert appeared. Gary touched the letter in his pocket and his mood darkened, like the sky before a sudden shower. He suddenly remembered the letter that Robert had written.

"You spelt 'progress' wrong and 'meeting'!" Gary barked at Robert.

"But it's worked, hasn't it. Told you it was a good idea," Robert was triumphant.

"No, it hasn't worked. My mum's given me a letter to give to Mr Doyle and it says, "Dear Mr Doyle, thanks for your recent letter . . ."

"You can lose that on the way to school," Robert said as if the letter was a chewing gum wrapper. "Just put it in that bin, there."

"No. Mum'll be furious!"

"She won't know. Tell Mr Doyle that she's coming up next Tuesday after school. He doesn't expect a reply to his letter."

"No – because he hasn't written one, stupid!"

Robert snatched the letter from Gary's pocket and stuffed it into a litter bin that was overflowing with the remnants of the previous night's takeaways. "Stop worrying, Gary. Cool it. Mr Doyle can never remember what he's written from one day to the next."

"I know but—"

"Look, Gary, all we want is for your mum and Mr Doyle to get together, like—"

"I know but what if she says, 'Did you get my letter?' and he says, 'What letter?' and she says—"

"Gary, I'm telling you it'll be safe. This time next week Mr Doyle will probably be buying popcorn for your mum at the new cineplex and you'll be getting ten out of ten all the time!"

"Yeah, I suppose," Gary sighed.

"You might even get into the school team – *and* we'll be getting free tickets for City matches. Trust me, Gary. It'll all work out brilliantly!"

SEVEN

It didn't work out brilliantly.

The following Tuesday, Bernadette kept her appointment with Mr Doyle.

Gary couldn't eat his tea that evening. He kept putting his hands over his face and cringing from the base of his stomach. What an embarrassment. No, it wasn't just one, it was a whole series of embarrassments.

Things had started to go seriously wrong after dinner – in Technology. Robert and Gary were designing a box for children's toothpaste. It had to be bright and appealing.

The whole class was working in twos and threes, so there was a steady buzz of 'working noise', as Mr Doyle called it, in the room. Mr Doyle moved from table to table, discussing the boxes and suggesting improvements.

"That's good!" he declared when he saw Gary's and Robert's work. "I like it." Mr Doyle squatted beside their table, his arms, head and shoulders just above the table top. "So, Gary, how's your mum?"

"Fine," Gary said, feeling awkward. "Thanks, Sir."

"And do you know what she wants to see me about? Any ideas, just so that I can be prepared?"

"It's just a general thing, isn't it, Gary?" Robert spoke quickly. Mr Doyle flashed a silencing look at Robert.

"Have you lost your tongue, Gary?"

"No, Sir, Robert's right. She wants to know how I'm progressing." He stared at Robert as he emphasised the last word.

"Good, so long as I know," Mr Doyle stood up, ready to move to the next desk.

"By the way, Sir," Robert said, quietly. "Gary's mum likes to be called Bernadette, or even Bernie. Doesn't she, Gary?"

Gary's mouth fell open. He was too amazed at Robert's advice to say anything.

"Thanks for telling me that, Trouble," Mr Doyle said. "Right then, I'll get on," he said with a bemused look.

"It's just that well, in the present circumstances, she doesn't really like being called Mrs McNab, does she Gary? Especially now that Mr McNab's thinking of getting married again. That's right, isn't it, Gary?"

Gary couldn't reply. It was a long time since he'd felt so strange.

Mum was busy with her paperwork, Gary was glad she was upstairs – and busy. She might forget about the afternoon appointment. Gary couldn't forget. He kept replaying the tape in his memory.

Robert and Gary sat in the reception area, waiting for Mum to finish. She didn't look happy after she emerged from the meeting. There was no twinkling eyes and smily smiles. "What is wrong with that man?" she questioned when they were safely clear of the school. "He's a right fruitcake!"

"What?" Gary and Robert spoke together, hardly believing their ears.

"He kept calling me *Bernie*! Can you believe that, Gary? You know how I hate being called that name."

"Honestly!" Robert sighed with mock indignation.

"He couldn't remember writing a letter, asking me to come to the school. He said he didn't recall receiving the one I wrote, and he wasn't sure why he'd asked me up to school in the first place! There's something fishy going on if you ask me. 'Call me Dermot' he said. The cheek of him!"

"He is handsome though, isn't he, Mrs McNab?" Robert said, gently.

"I don't know what's up with him, Gary," she said, ignoring Robert's remark.

"He's a very good football coach, Mrs McNab. Isn't he, Gary?"

"Well, I'm glad you're impressed, Robert. Did you hand that letter in, Gary?"

"Yes Mum," Gary said, his fingers crossed deep inside his pocket.

"Do you know, Mrs McNab, I think he likes you," Robert said confidently.

"Does he indeed," Bernadette said, still grim-faced.

"He's always asking about you, isn't he Gary? And when you came into school with Gary's kit the other week, he looked well pleased, didn't he Gary?"

"Yes," Gary muttered. He felt extremely uncomfortable.

"Maybe he just wrote that note so he had an excuse to see you," Robert suggested.

Bernadette began to smile. "I doubt it, somehow," she said, amused in spite of herself by Robert's suggestions.

"I was wondering, I hope you don't mind me asking, did he ask you out, Mrs McNab?"

"*What*?" Bernadette stopped and peered closely at Robert.

Gary wanted to die, there and then. He wanted to be on another continent so that he wouldn't have to look at the amazed expression on his mum's face. He knew the rage that could follow that startled look.

"I was just wondering if he'd asked you to go to that new cineplex with him," Robert asked uncertainly.

"Robert. If I wasn't in such a foul mood with Mr 'Call-me-Dermot' Doyle, I would walk you straight to your house and tell your mother how cheeky you've been!"

"Sorry Mrs McNab, I didn't mean to be cheeky. My mum says he'd be quite a catch," Robert added in a chatty tone.

That's when the bleep went off, saving Robert from the razor-sharp edge of Bernadette's tongue.

"Come on, Gary. Let's get home quickly. I have to get to a phone – see whose baby is about to arrive."

"So, how am I progressing, Mum?" Gary asked, casting a filthy look at Robert.

"Does the whole school know our business, Gary? There's nothing that annoys me more than a sympathetic teacher who says, 'I know what you're going through, Bernie,'

Ooh – that man!"

Gary scraped all of his tea into the bin. His mum still wasn't any good at cooking and he wasn't hungry. The phone rang. "You're right, Gary." It was Robert. "Your mum and Mr Doyle aren't really suited, are they? We'll have to think of something else. Shame though – he could have got loads of free tickets for—"

Gary did not want to talk to Robert. He just mumbled, "Bye," and hung up the phone.

Even before his mum had finished her paperwork, Gary went to bed. Tired, depressed and dreading the next day at school, he climbed the stairs. Finding a new dad wasn't going to be easy.

"Funny," he thought. "Mr Doyle doesn't look like a Dermot."

EIGHT

On Wednesday, Dermot Doyle was in a dreadful mood. "Something must have upset him," Robert whispered. "Maybe he's discovered that we tried to fix him up with your mum."

"Gary McNab. Stop talking this minute!" Mr Doyle boomed.

"I wasn't—" Gary stuttered.

"No, you never are. It's always the other person, isn't it?" Mr Doyle said, sarcastically. "It's always somebody else's fault, isn't it?"

Gary wanted to shout, "If you'd open your eyes and look carefully you would see that it was Robert talking and not me!" Instead he mumbled, "Yes, Sir. Sorry, Sir."

After dinner they raced into the classroom hot and tired from playing football. Mr Doyle pulled Robert and Gary aside and hissed, "You might think you're dead clever, but I know you two are up to something and I don't like it." Maybe he had found out.

The afternoon dragged on as though it was a cold, rainy Monday with spelling and arithmetic tests.

Back home, Bernadette knew something was wrong when she saw Gary divide his tea into quarters and then eighths. "Doing fractions at school?" she asked, smiling, teasing Gary into a response even though he seemed miles away.

"No," Gary sighed.

"Well, what is it, love? Don't you like the way I lovingly peeled the outer wrappings and placed this delicious Seafood Surprise in the microwave?"

Gary couldn't help smiling. "Mum," he asked in a drawn-out way. "Can I ask you something? Do you mind?"

Bernadette placed her fork to one side of her unfinished meal and listened. "What is it, love?"

"It's just that, me and Robert were talking and— Well, you know how Dad's met Karen?"

"Yes."

"Well . . . do you think you'll ever meet anyone else? And what will happen to me if—"

"Oh, Gary, love," she said gently. "How am I likely to meet anybody – the job I'm doing? The only men I meet are doting fathers of brand new babies and bossy doctors."

"But what if— Would you like to meet someone else?" Gary asked.

"Not really, Gary. I've sort of got used to me and you in this house. I like the space. It's nice, isn't it? We can choose what we want to do or where to go. We don't need anyone else, do we?"

"Do you think that Dad will ever come back?" Gary asked suddenly.

"And bring Karen with him?" Mum laughed. "No, Gary, there's no point believing in fairy tales or happy endings. Your dad won't be coming back. He wants to marry Karen. He still loves *you*, though. He really cares for you, so don't be worrying about that."

"I wish—" Gary started to speak.

"So do I, Gary."

There was a long, uneasy silence in the room. It was broken only by Gary's mother gently tapping her fork against the plate. "You know why this is called Seafood Surprise, don't you?" Bernadette asked. "The surprise is: there's no seafood in it!"

"Mum, how did you meet Dad?" Gary asked, ignoring his mother's efforts to make him laugh.

"Oh, Gary! What's that got to do with Seafood Surprise?" Bernadette said, avoiding the question.

"Nothing. I was just wondering."

"It's one of those wondering days, isn't it, Gary Tell you what, how do you fancy going to the new cineplex?"

"Yesss! What to see?"

"Anything. Let's pick a number and go to that screen, we'll see what's on when we get there. Come on, let's go. I've had a hard day, too, love."

The cinema was almost empty as they sat chewing popcorn and looking at the closed screen curtains. Gary was pleased that they were out of the house. It could feel small with the two of them there. Smaller than when Dad was there. He was feeling better already.

"Remember what I asked you earlier?" Gary said, reminding his mum.

"About fractions?"

"No! About Dad?"

"Oh, that. What did you want to know?"

"Well, how *did* you meet Dad?" Gary asked again. He felt that this was much easier than talking at home. He didn't have to look at his mum and no one else could hear. There only seemed to be two other women in the cinema. They sat near the front and talked quickly and furiously, in between scoopfuls of ice-cream.

Gary wanted to have some clue about how he and Robert could find another man for his mum.

"Same as a lot of people, Gary. In a nightclub. Haven't I ever told you about it?" Bernadette's words broke into Gary's thoughts. She didn't wait for an answer. "No, I don't suppose I have. Mind you, you've never asked before. I was on holiday with my friends in Greece. I met your dad on the second night there. He asked me out for a meal, you know. We went to a restaurant where the waiter only knew two words in English. It was during the World Cup. What do you think the two words were?"

"Hello and goodbye?" Gary suggested.

"No! When we said that we were English, the waiter said, 'Ah, Gary Lineker!' Your dad and I couldn't stop laughing. It was brilliant. Between every course he'd come up to the table and say, 'Gary Lineker, Gary Lineker'. Actually, I think that's why we called you Gary."

"After Gary Lineker?"

"Yes. He's a nice person to be named after, isn't he?"

"Why don't you do that again, Mum? Why don't you go to a nightclub and meet someone else?" Gary asked. He needed to be sure that this time he and Robert wouldn't be wasting their time.

"Because I'm too old for all that. That's for young people. Besides which, Gary, I don't want to meet anyone else. Look, the film's about to start. You don't mind seeing *The Lion King* for the second time, do you?"

The lights dimmed, the curtains opened and the bright adverts filled the cinema with music and flashing images.

"Looking for the person of your dreams?" a woman asked. She looked a bit like Karen – all make-up and hair.

"Or nightmares," Gary said.

His mum laughed. "Funny place to be if you're looking for a dream person. You wouldn't see them in the dark!"

"Are you searching for the perfect partner? Then look in your weekend paper for details of our special spring offer. We can find the perfect partner for you!"

"That's a good idea," Gary thought, looking at his mum.

In the cinema semi-darkness he noticed her gazing wistfully at the photos in her purse. Photos of when they were a family. Before Karen.

If it wasn't for Karen, he wouldn't need to find a man for his mum.

NINE

Robert was off school for the rest of that week. Gary joined in with Kieran Sackville and his friends on the small field but it wasn't the same.

"Have a good day, Gary?" his mum asked one evening.

"Not bad. Robert's off. He must be sick," Gary replied.

"Oh, yes, I met his gran in the Post Office. She was saying Robert's got an ear infection. Who did you play with then?"

"Kieran and Danny Shah and all that crowd," Gary said.

Bernadette was tackling the ironing as if it was a centre forward for your worst enemy's team. "Good," she said, smoothing the creases out of one of her work dresses.

"Did Robert's gran say when he'd be back?"

"No. We were having a bit of a laugh, actually, Gary. We were talking about matchmakers."

Gary's mum stood the iron to one side and leaned back. "She said Robert's got a bit of a thing about them at the moment."

Gary began to sweat. At first his mouth wouldn't work. Bernadette didn't notice. She was too busy with an awkward pair of jeans.

"I wonder if everything's all right with Robert's mum and Ronan. I haven't seen them for ages."

"They're away a lot," Gary said, quickly. "With Ronan's lorry." Gary was glad his mum didn't look up from her ironing.

First thing on Saturday Gary cycled around to Robert's house. "Your gran's been talking to my mum about matchmakers," Gary said, accusingly. "What have you been saying?"

"Nothing." Robert shuffled about on his chair. "Gran saw this in the free paper." He pulled a crumpled page from his pocket, ignoring Gary's angry tone.

PERFECT PARTNERS

Searching for your Soul Mate?
Hankering after your Other Half?
Pining for your Perfect Partner?

Then look no further.

Fill in the details below and
we'll help you with your search.

"What's school been like?" Robert asked as Gary read the full page advert for Perfect Partners.

"Not bad. There was an advert at the pictures about this."

"Have I missed anything?"

"Oh, yes. Dermot's helping to run a one-day soccer school – 'Play the Tyrone Bradley way'."

"When?" Robert asked, eagerly.

"In about a fortnight."

"Will Tyrone Bradley be there?" Robert asked.

"Dermot says he's trying to arrange it but if not, his personal trainer will be."

"Wicked! I'm going, are you, Gary?"

"Yes. If Dermot lets us, after what we did."

"That's a point. But what about this, then? Are we going to fill it in for your mum?" Robert said, shaking the crumpled paper.

Gary ignored the question and asked, "Has your infection gone? I don't want to catch anything and miss the football day."

Robert breathed heavily and coughed. "No," he said in a hoarse whisper. "And it's a deadly virus."

"Don't be stupid," Gary shouted. "I'm not stopping if you're still spreading germs."

"Some friend you are! Look, are we filling in this form for your mum or not?"

Gary was in a bad mood and he didn't feel like it but he looked carefully at the Perfect Partners application form.

PERFECT PARTNERS

Making Dreams Come True

Tell us about yourself by ticking the boxes that apply to you so that we can find your perfect partner!

Are you:

shy .... ☐

extrovert .... ☐

out-going .... ☐

confident .... ☐

quiet .... ☐

fun-loving .... ☐

a non-smoker ....☐

18 – 24 .... ☐

25 – 30 .... ☐

31 – 40 .... ☐

41 – 50 .... ☐

over 50 .... ☐

male .... ☐

female .... ☐

Do you like:

reading .... ☐

cinema .... ☐

theatre .... ☐

music .... ☐

poetry .... ☐

gardening .... ☐

needlework ....☐

politics .... ☐

sport .... ☐

cooking .... ☐

entertaining ...☐

watching TV ...☐

eating out .... ☐

Complete this form and send it to the address below.

We can make your dream come true.

They sat at the big table in Robert's dining room for ages, looking blankly at the form.

"What's extrovert?" Robert asked.

"Sort of loud and always talking to people, I think," Gary replied.

"We'll tick that. Your mum's an extrovert."

"No she isn't, she's not loud!"

"All right, calm down! Shall we say she's outgoing then?"

"And fun loving," Gary added. "Tick twenty-five to thirty, then we won't get someone who's too old."

They stared long and hard at the list of interests. "What does your mum like?" Robert asked with a sigh.

"Delivering babies and talking."

"They're not on the list. Let's tick sport," Robert suggested.

"But she hates sport," Gary insisted.

"I know, I know but we have to find her someone who likes the same things as us, otherwise you won't get on," Robert said. "Let's tick cooking and eating out as well."

"She can't cook for— She can't even cook ready-cooked pizzas!"

"I know, I know but no one will be interested in her if she's no good at cooking."

"That's daft. That's pure daft," Gary said, shaking his head.

Over an hour later, the form was ready to post. Bernadette McNab had become an extroverted, fun-loving woman whose interests were: sport, cooking, eating out and watching television.

As the form dropped into the post box, Gary felt as though a stone had fallen to the bottom of his stomach. What had they done? What if his mum ever found out?

TEN

When the reply from Perfect Partners eventually dropped on to the mat at Robert's address, he didn't notice. For the first few days after they'd sent the form, Robert had got up ridiculously early and waited expectantly for the post. Then he got bored. Now he had other things on his mind.

It was exactly a fortnight later, the day of Dermot Doyle's Soccer School with Tyrone Bradley. Gary and Robert were almost sick with excitement. Nothing else in the world mattered. They had even forgotten all about Perfect Partners.

Mrs Bryant collected the letters that morning. She wasn't too surprised to see a letter addressed to Mrs Bernadette McNab. Years ago, when Robert and Gary had been at nursery together, she had been friends with Bernadette. Sometimes they would order clothes or books

60

from catalogues and have them sent to one another's address. Bernadette had said she didn't want Eugene to know how much she'd spent on clothes or books.

That had been before Bernadette had become so engrossed in her work. It was even before Gary's dad had left home.

"Robert, I'm going to nip in and see Gary's mum on the way home today. Haven't seen her for ages. Tell Gary, won't you?"

"Yes, Mum." Robert was hardly listening. His gaze was fixed on the last slice of toast. Ronan would have it if Robert wasn't careful.

"I have to take her this letter." Mrs Bryant smoothed the letter beside her plate. Robert continued to stare at the toast. "Funny pink envelope with P.P. I wonder what that stands for? Strange name for a catalogue company."

Something suddenly clicked in Robert's brain. "What?" he shouted, jumping manically out of his chair.

"I'm just saying about this letter for Gary's mum. It's ages since she ordered anything from a catalogue and it's not as if she needs to send it here. Gary's dad's not living there anymore—"

"I'll take it," Robert interrupted hurriedly.

"No, no. Don't you worry about it, love. I'll pop around there this evening. Haven't seen Bernadette for—"

"She won't be in. She never is. She works nearly all the time. I'll take it!" Robert tried to snatch the letter from beside his mum's plate. Mrs Bryant slowly wafted the letter out of Robert's reach. Ronan took the last slice of toast.

Robert wanted to shout, "You greedy pig!" at Ronan and, "Give me that letter!" at his mum. Instead he slumped back into his chair.

"Poor old Gary. It's no wonder he spends so much time around here, Robert. You don't realise how lucky you are, having Gran here all the time." Mrs Bryant continued.

"Shall I take the letter then?" Robert asked, pleased that this story had been believed.

Ronan smiled his sickly smile at Robert. Robert wished, for the thousandth time, that his mum had met a City footballer.

"Look at the time!" Mrs Bryant announced. "I'm late. Ronan you'll have to drop me off." In her rush, the letter to Bernadette was forgotten.

Robert hugged the letter to his chest and breathed a huge sigh of relief.

Robert should have realised that this wasn't going to be a good day. Tyrone Bradley didn't appear at the Soccer School. Neither did his personal trainer. "Bit of a crisis, I'm afraid," Mr Doyle said. "City aren't too happy with the way he's playing and he's been having some bad publicity lately, so he couldn't be here."

They watched a video of Tyrone Bradley's super skills and then tried to copy him. Only half the football team stayed. At break time Gary and Robert ran behind the Portakabin that served as the school music room. "It's the letter from P.P. – Perfect Partners!" Robert said, waving it about.

"Well, let's open it then," Gary said, excitedly tearing at the envelope.

PERFECT PARTNERS
Meeting in the Modern Sense
Making Dreams Come True

Dear Bernadette,
Let me introduce myself to you. My name is Tamsin and I'm responsible for the new members of our dating agency. I would like to welcome you aboard!

Since our introduction agency was established five years ago, we have become one of the region's leading places to meet friends and future partners. I have lost count of the number of weddings I've attended in the last year and two of our clients have recently celebrated the birth of their third child. Success indeed!

So you see, our business goes from strength to strength or should I say marriage to marriage! The difference between **PERFECT PARTNERS** and other agencies is that we are local and we *care* about our clients.

Bernadette, we have found a man for you! He's just a little older than you are and has one child and a good job. I must say, yours seems like a perfect match.

If you would like to meet the mystery man we would ask you to send a cheque for £55.

On receipt of your cheque I will send you the name, box number and telephone number of your prospective perfect partner, as well as a list of other suitable candidates. We strongly urge our clients to meet in a public place. Always tell your family where you are going and what time you are expected to return.

Thank you for your interest in our agency. I look forward hearing from you very soon.

Your friend,

Tamsin
Perfect Partners

"Fifty-five pounds! Fifty-five!" Robert shouted. Where are we going to get that from? What a waste of money!"

"Yes," Gary said quietly.

"It was a real drag getting up in the middle of the night to make sure that I got your mum's letter before anyone else found it. I don't want to have to do that forever. Anyway, you could see City play five times for that much money!"

Robert continued to fume about the expense of a dating agency. It was a waste of money as far as he was concerned. Robert wanted to drop the idea. They could think of something better.

"I'm not sure if—" Gary began.

"If what? If you want to pay all that money? I don't blame you. If it was my mum I wouldn't," Robert said, continuing to rage.

"No, it's not that. I'm not sure if I even want my mum to get married again," Gary said, surprising even himself.

"What? I wish you'd make up your mind!"

"I'm not sure. I don't really know," Gary said. The letter had made him feel so strange and sad. Like the day Karen sat outside the house in a van, chewing gum, waiting for his dad.

"They don't have to get married, you know, Gary. My mum and Ronan haven't."

"I don't know, I'm not sure," Gary almost whispered.

"What shall I do with this, then?" Robert asked, waving the letter about. "Shall I chuck it out?"

"Yes," Gary said, flatly. "Chuck it out." That should have been the end of the matter. But it wasn't.

ELEVEN

A few days later, another letter addressed to Bernadette arrived at Robert's house. This time he collected the mail from the front door and spotting the Perfect Partners envelope, he stuffed it into his pocket.

"Shall I throw it away?" he asked Gary later.

"No. Let's have a look first," Gary said, overcome with curiosity.

PERFECT PARTNERS
Meeting in the Modern Sense
Making Dreams Come True

Dear Friend,
　　　This year we celebrate the
　　　21st Anniversary
　　　of our Agency.
Are you still looking for that special

person? Now's the time to join our agency. For a limited period of 21 days our fees have been reduced to **£21.00**.

Apply now for this special, special offer.

We are *so* looking forward to hearing from you.

Tamsin
Perfect Partners

"That's brilliant!" Gary almost jumped about with excitement. "It's a reduction of thirty-four pounds!"

"But it's still twenty-one pounds. That's way out of our league. It's too much!"

"I might have enough money in my money-box," Gary said, hopefully.

Robert was about to disagree when he noticed Mr Doyle walking towards their table. "Dermot's coming," he hissed. Gary shuffled forwards in his seat so that the letter from Perfect Partners was hidden.

"How are your pictures coming on, lads?" Mr Doyle asked.

"Fine," Robert and Gary said together. They were designing a new cover for *Danny, the Champion of the World*.

"I want your new cover to reflect the close relationship between father and son," Mr Doyle had said earlier.

Mr Doyle hovered behind Gary and Robert as if sensing that something was going on. "Sir, just out of interest," Robert began. "If you needed, say, twenty-one pounds from your mum and dad, how would you ask for it? What would you say?"

"Depends," Mr Doyle said, thoughtfully. "What's it for?"

"Gary wants to buy a present for his mum."

"No I don't! You want to buy something for your mum," Gary protested.

Mr Doyle, looking puzzled, hesitated. Then he said, "Why don't you ask your dad for the money?" as though it was a plainly obvious solution.

The two fell into silence as they completed their cover designs. Gary thought about how he would ask his dad. It wouldn't be a lie. After all, it was a present for his mum.

As soon as Mr Doyle was back at the front of the classroom, Gary stuffed the Perfect Partners letter into his bag. It was quite safe there – as far as his mum was concerned his bag was strictly private.

Gary and Robert were surprised to see Bernadette standing at the school gate. "What's up, Mum?" Gary asked, slightly irritated that she had come to meet him.

"Nothing. I just wanted to see my lovely boy." She said, trying to embrace Gary. He squirmed, Robert laughed. At the main road, he ran off towards his home.

"It's a bit embarrassing, Mum, meeting me from school," Gary said.

"Is it love? I'm sorry. I'm just a bit fed-up." Gary didn't reply. "I rang your dad to check up about this weekend. See if you were still going to see City on Saturday."

"Oh? What did he say?"

"He wasn't there," Bernadette said, quietly. "I had a little chat with Karen, Gary. She seemed to take great delight in telling me . . ." She took a deep breath before continuing. "They've set a wedding date." After a few moments Bernadette whispered. "What a dreadful day!"

"Don't say that, Mum," Gary said. "Things will get better, I promise. Just wait and see." And he gave her a quick hug.

"They're having a really big *do*. It'll cost them a fortune."

As Bernadette continued to talk about the plans for the dreaded wedding, Gary decided that he *would* ask his dad for twenty-one pounds. If they had all that money to spend on a big wedding, it was the least he could do for his mum.

On Saturday, Gary went to see City with his

dad as usual. The wedding wasn't mentioned. They were too busy complaining about how City had wasted good money on Tyrone Bradley who was playing football like somebody sleepwalking.

"Can I have some money, Dad?" Gary asked at half-time.

"Oh, that sounds a bit ominous," Eugene said. "What's it for?"

"I want to buy a present for Mum – cheer her up a bit." It isn't a lie, it isn't a lie. Gary kept repeating to himself.

"Good idea, son. How much do you want?"

Eugene McNab cringed slightly when Gary told him the amount. "How much, son? Twenty pounds? What are you buying her, a pearl necklace?"

"I can't tell you, Dad, but I promise I'm going to spend it all on Mum," Gary replied.

Two days later, Gary and Robert delivered the money and form to Perfect Partners. Their offices were on a small side street at the back of the main shopping centre, in between a run-down cafe and a boarded-up shop. It looked horrible. Gary found it hard to believe that dreams could come true on this street.

"Shall we leave it?" Gary asked. "It looks awful."

"Don't look, just do it," Robert said. "Hurry up, Gary. Your mum isn't going to live here or anything after she gets married. Just get on with it or we'll be dead late home."

Gary posted the letter along with the money. As they reached the end of the street, Gary looked back at the Perfect Partners office. He saw a woman leaving. She looked about ninety. "That must be Tamsin," he said quietly. His stomach turned over.

"I've done the wrong thing," he said, almost in a whisper. "What will my mum say if she ever found out?"

"She won't, Gary," Robert said, confidently. "Trust me."

TWELVE

PERFECT PARTNERS
Meeting in the Modern Sense
Making Dreams Come True

Dear Bernadette,
I am delighted that you have decided to meet up with the man of your dreams. We hope that you will bring one another happiness for many years.

Your chosen partner is:

Mr Matt Rossi,
P.O. Box 3751,
Oakesthorpe.
Tel. 9287565

We will leave it to you to arrange a meeting with Mr Rossi. When doing so, Bernadette, remember:

   1 Meet in a public place.

   2 Tell your family where you are going.

   3 Tell someone what time you expect to return.

   4 Make your first meeting in the middle of the day.

Once again, I thank you for your interest in our agency. May I wish you all the very best for your future happiness.

Your friend,

Tamsin

Gary and Robert had several tries at writing a letter to Matt Rossi.

Dear Matt,
My name is Bernadette McNab. I deliver babies for a living. I never meet any men in my job and that's why I'm going through Perfect Partners. I have one son, Gary. He is a lovely boy.
Write soon.

Dear Matt,
I look forward to meeting up with you soon. I will have to bring my son with me as I cannot find a babysitter. Also, he worries about me if I go out by myself at night. (Or even during the day.)
See you soon.

"There's coffee cake on the table, lads," Robert's gran shouted.

"She probably wants to know what we're up to," Robert said, removing the letters from the computer screen.

"She is a bit nosy, your gran," Gary said. "But in a nice way," he added, noticing Robert's annoyed look.

"We could ask her how to write a proper letter," Robert suggested.

"Don't say anything about Perfect Partners, will you?" Gary pleaded.

"Well, lads, how's the matchmaking going?" Robert's gran asked as they started to tuck into the coffee cake.

"Terrible," Robert said.

"You mustn't be doing it right," she said, appearing to lose interest.

"How do you write a letter to someone you don't know very well, Gran?" Robert asked.

"Is this for the matchmaking?" Robert's gran asked. She was smiling broadly and her eyes were twinkling. "Are you doing it on the computer? Well, why don't I come up and help you. Sure, I've nothing better to do."

"No, no, that's all right," Gary said, flashing a warning look at Robert. "We'd like to know how to write it, it's more for school than for the matchmaking. Mr Doyle asked us to do it, didn't he, Robert?"

"Ah, well, if it's for Mr Doyle – he is a lovely man. I often say to your mother, Robert, wouldn't it be great if she'd met someone like him years ago. Sure, he'd be a great catch for anyone! He's not married, you know, Gary."

Gary and Robert looked blankly at his gran as she raved on about Dermot. They could no longer see the attraction.

"Sorry, lads, I'm going on a bit, aren't I? Why wouldn't I help you? Pass us a bit of paper and I'll show you what to do."

You put your address here.

Then the date.

Put their address, here.

"Then start:"

Dear xxxx

So they did.

P.O. Box 12,
32, Ramsey Grove,
Leicester.

Mr Matt Rossi,
P.O. Box 3752,
Oakesthorpe.

Dear Matt Rossi,

I would like to arrange a meeting. I am writing to you because I find it hard talking to people on the phone. I am quite shy. My son, Gary could be quite difficult about me meeting up with a man. When we meet we will have to make it look as though we have bumped into each other by accident. If he knows we have met through a dating agency he will be very upset. We can meet up in the Castle Gardens next Sunday. I quite often go there for a walk with my son. I will wear a yellow top and navy blue trousers. I will have to pretend that I don't know you for a while, just to convince my son. We will be walking through the Castle Gardens between three and four o'clock. Normally, we sit down for a while as my son likes to explore next to the river. Be careful what you say. My son must not know about this so we have to make it look as though we met by chance.

See you on Sunday.
Bernadette (McNab)

P.S. My son will probably bring a friend with him.
P.P.S. Whatever you do, don't say <u>anything</u> about Perfect Partners.

THIRTEEN

The following Sunday, it was pouring with rain. It wasn't the gentle sort of drizzle which annoys you when you're playing football. No, the rain beat at the house, lashing the doors and the windows and the gates, daring anyone to venture out.

"It'll probably be sunny by this afternoon," Bernadette McNab said when Gary told her the weather was making him depressed.

It wasn't. Gary was furious. "You shouldn't get upset about the weather, Gary," his mum advised. "It's way beyond our control. Anyways, 'April showers bring May flowers'."

Gary wanted to scream. This wasn't a shower, it was a monsoon! Still, the arrangements had been made and he didn't want to disappoint Matt Rossi.

"Mum, you haven't forgotten you promised

to take me and Robert to the Castle Gardens?" Gary said in a pleading tone.

"You're joking aren't you? In this terrible weather?" said Bernadette. "What is so special about the Castle Gardens that makes you want to go there on such a dreadful day?"

"I want to see how the river is coping with all the rain. See if it bursts its banks," Gary replied, hesitantly.

Then, he had the almost impossible task of persuading his mother to wear her navy trousers and yellow top. He knew Matt Rossi wouldn't miss her in that outfit. "I'll put my long green mac on," Bernadette said as she tidied the hallway.

"No don't!" Gary shouted. "You don't need a coat, we'll take a big umbrella." Gary couldn't remember the last time he'd had to beg his mum to do something. By the time they arrived at the Castle Gardens under a vast golfing umbrella, he felt exhausted.

There were only three other people in the Castle Gardens. An old man who clung to the seat next to the gate. He drank from a bottle covered by a plastic, supermarket carrier, apparently unaware of the torrential rain. Then there were Matt and Francesca Rossi. She was a girl of about eight years old.

Matt Rossi walked casually towards

Bernadette, Gary and Robert. His daughter moved a round lollipop from cheek to cheek and stared out angrily at the rain.

"We must be mad!" Matt Rossi announced, looking towards the empty factories on the far side of the river. "Being out in this weather," he turned to look at Bernadette.

"Yes," she replied distantly. Then she began to walk away.

Matt Rossi looked distinctly puzzled. He watched as the three of them walked towards the river. Gary glared at Robert, desperately hoping he would think of a way to make his mum carry on talking.

"Do you mind if we have a look at the old landing stage, Mrs McNab?" Robert asked.

"I don't know, Robert. Be careful."

Robert and Gary stepped down on to the landing stage. "Watch this," he whispered.

"What are you doing." Gary hissed.

Within a few seconds, Robert's foot seemed to be trapped between an old barge and the landing stage. He cried out, "Help, I've caught my foot! Aah! Mrs McNab, you'll have to get help!"

"You stupid— What have you done that for?" Gary shouted.

"Oh, my God, Robert! What's the matter?" Bernadette said, clearly distressed. She was panicking and unable to think straight.

"Get that man, Mrs McNab!" Robert said, his face creased with pain. "He'll have to pull me out!"

"He can't help, he's drunk!" Bernadette said, desperately.

"Not him. The other one over there with the girl!"

"Excuse me, excuse me!" Bernadette shouted. "Help! My son's friend is trapped on the landing stage and he's in great—"

Matt Rossi ran over to the edge of the river, followed slowly by a surly Francesca. "Don't worry," he called gallantly. "We'll soon have you out of there."

Within a few minutes Robert's foot had been released. "I think I'll be all right," he said, limping along. As Bernadette turned to thank Matt Rossi, Robert winked at Gary.

"Are you all right?" Matt Rossi asked Bernadette. "You look terribly shaken."

"Well, it was a bit of a shock," Bernadette began.

"Tell you what. We could all do with a cup of hot, strong, sweet tea. I think there's somewhere open on the High Street," Matt Rossi suggested.

Bernadette breathed a sigh of relief. "Thank you so much for your help. What would we have done if you hadn't been here?"

A confused look crossed Matt Rossi's face. "Well—"

"Shall we go for that hot drink?" Robert asked, interrupting Matt Rossi. "I think I need something, Mrs McNab."

Gary and Robert dawdled behind Bernadette McNab and Matt Rossi as they headed for the café. "Are you all right now?" Gary inquired.

"I wasn't stuck," Robert said, smiling. "I pulled the barge towards me when Matt Rossi came down."

"You're mad!" Gary said.

"Well, we had to do something, your mum obviously wanted to go home."

Francesca, who was even further behind, caught up with Robert and Gary. "I'm going to tell my dad, ugly! You weren't stuck," Francesca said.

"Shut up, you little squirt," Robert snapped.

"Or you'll spoil everything," Gary hissed.

"What do you mean, fishface? 'Spoil everything'?" Francesca asked.

"Nothing. It's none of your business!" Robert said.

"My dad is desperate to meet another woman," she announced. "And he's after your mum now!" she said to Gary.

"I wish *you* were stuck on that barge. Permanently!" Gary hissed.

Gary and Robert laughed and ran a little to catch up with Matt Rossi and Bernadette, but slowed when they remembered Robert was supposed to have a limp. In the café, Robert and Gary had to sit on a separate table as there wasn't room for them next to Matt Rossi, Francesca and Bernadette.

They said goodbye at the town end of Castle Gardens. "What a nice man," Gary's mum said as they drove home. "He works at the hospital, too. What a coincidence!" Gary and Robert smiled at one another gleefully.

But, for Gary and Robert, there was one big problem – Francesca.

FOURTEEN

It was Monday morning break – a very bright, sunny day. The weekend rain had given a sort of polished look to the playground. Gary and Robert kicked a ball about next to the music Portakabin.

"What if—" Gary said as he dribbled the ball towards the two coats acting as goal posts.

"What?" Robert replied, all the time watching Gary's feet in case he was about to shoot.

"What if Matt Rossi mentions Perfect Partners? You know, when him and my mum are talking."

"He won't," Robert said. "Come on, shoot!"

Gary had stopped moving about. His right foot rested on the ball and he looked towards the sky, watching the vapour trail of a passing jet as he thought. "He might! And then we're in trouble."

"Give us the ball," Robert said, impatiently. "They won't talk about it. They'll talk about their jobs and their kids and then about films and sport. That is if they ever meet up again."

"I wonder if they arranged to see one another?" Gary said, moving the ball slightly. He couldn't stop thinking about the scene in the Castle Gardens the day before.

"Well, we won't know unless your mum says something," Robert said. "You can't ask her or she'll be suspicious."

For days and days Bernadette never mentioned anything about the incident in the Castle Gardens. Gary couldn't help thinking that the whole episode had been a waste of twenty-one pounds. "What a complete waste of money," he kept saying.

"You don't know yet," Robert said, trying to reassure him.

Then, almost a week later, as Bernadette emptied out her briefcase she announced, "Hey, Gary, you'll never guess who I bumped into."

"Who?" By this time Gary had almost forgotten about Matt Rossi.

"Do you remember that nice man who rescued Robert in the Castle Garden?"

"Where did you see him?"

"Well, he works at the hospital. We've arranged to meet for lunch tomorrow. He is such a nice, chatty, interesting man. It'll do me good."

Gary's thoughts drifted away as his mum talked about Matt Rossi. Although he was pleased that the money hadn't been wasted, it felt strange to hear his mum talk like this.

"Brilliant!" Robert said, when he heard the news the next day. "It's working."

"He's Italian. Well, Italian descent, Gary, hence the name Rossi. He works part-time so that he can look after his little girl. You'd like him, he's mad about football," Bernadette said after their lunch date. "He wants us all to get together sometime – me, you, Matt and his little girl, Francesca."

"She's a brat, Mum!"

"How do you know?" Bernadette asked, slightly crestfallen.

"That Sunday, in the rain. Remember?"

"Ah, that's different. That was a miserable day. He loves his little girl, you know. He talks about her so much. I like that. I'm sure I bore people silly talking about you, Gary."

Gary looked closely at his mum as she talked and talked about Matt Rossi. Her eyes really twinkled and she smiled constantly. It was like Robert's gran had said. But Gary wasn't happy about it. He should have been. On paper, Matt Rossi would have made a good substitute for his dad. He liked football, too.

Gary tried to talk to Robert about it. Robert didn't understand. "What's up with you, Gary? We've cracked it. We've found someone for your mum and you should be dead happy!" Robert was impatient with Gary's doubts.

"Yes, but— What if Matt Rossi talks about how they met?"

"He won't. Anyway, he's probably forgotten by now," Robert said.

"But what if he does? And what about Francesca?"

Robert didn't know what to say to that. No amount of scheming would make Francesca disappear. Besides, that wasn't what was really bothering Gary.

"Are you going to tell Dad?" Gary asked his mum one evening as she was poring over her paperwork.

"Tell him what, love?"

"About that man – Matt Rossi?"

"No. There's no need. Don't worry, Gary. There's absolutely nothing in it."

"But you've seen him about five times now," Gary said.

"I know, but there's absolutely no reason to tell your dad."

Within a week, Gary's mum had changed her mind.

FIFTEEN

Bernadette stood at the back door staring at two sparrows fighting over a crust she'd put out for them. Gary rushed about, filling his rucksack with sandwiches, a tennis ball and last night's homework. It was a few minutes before he realised that his mum seemed rooted to the spot.

"Mum, where are my P.E. shorts?" Gary asked.

"Wherever you left them," his mum whispered.

"I left them in the wash basket to be washed," Gary said.

"Well, I'm afraid they will still be there."

Gary slumped on to the settee. What was up with his mother? He was the one who suffered if he didn't have any clean P.E. shorts.

This had happened before, when Dad had left. The washing piled up in a great heap at the top of the stairs. Gary had had to wear the same clothes for ages. Now here she was, forgetting the washing all over again.

"Your dad sent this," Bernadette McNab said, passing a pink envelope to Gary. He had an idea what it was.

"Is it an invite, Mum?" he said, without opening the envelope. His dad had already told him about the dreaded event.

"Yes. Don't you want to look at it?"

Gary slowly removed the pink card from the envelope.

Eugene and Karen
invite you to
their wedding
at Leicester Registry Office
on
June 30th at 2.30 p.m.
RSVP

"I hope it rains!" Gary said.

"Heavily!" his mum added. Then she laughed, but it wasn't like a proper laugh. "I remember, when we sent out our wedding invitations."

"Did you have many guests?" Gary asked. This was something he had never thought of – his mum and dad's wedding.

"Lots and lots." Now she sounded serious again. After a few minutes she said, "Shall we go, Gary? You'd have to get something to wear."

"Well, I don't want to go. No way! I can't stand Karen!" Gary said.

"She'll be your stepmother, son."

Stepmother. Stepmother. Gary said the word over and over in his mind and as he said it, he began to realise exactly what was happening.

He heard his dad's words again. "I'll still be your dad." Gary wanted to scream at him. He wanted to shake his shoulders and say, "Yes, but you never said anything about a *stepmother!*"

On the way to school, every ant was Karen. Gary stamped on each one and shouted her name. It made him feel better.

She was always polite, Karen, and she could cook brilliant roast dinners and keep everything hot. But he still hated eating at that house. He felt as if it was betraying his mum.

Gary was on his mum's side. That's how it became – sides. Like playing football. He still liked his dad but he was on his mum's side and Karen knew that.

That's why Karen was so careful about what she said to Gary. She knew everything would be reported back to Bernadette – because you always stick up for those who are on your side.

Mum's side and Dad's side. Now it looked as

though Mum might have somebody else on her side, thanks to Gary and Robert.

But Gary wasn't sure if he wanted Matt Rossi on his side. It was so, so hard, trying to find the right man for Mum.

SIXTEEN

The following Saturday, Gary went to see City with his dad. Once again, City were unable to win and their new star, Tyrone Bradley, played like a donkey. Gary felt really unhappy.

After they'd driven home from the match, Mum suddenly appeared at the driver's window. "Can you come in for five minutes, Eugene?" This was the first time since Gary had returned from the adventure holiday that Dad had been in the house.

"Take the weight off your feet, love," Gary's mum said as Eugene hovered in the hall. He walked into the back room and sat nervously at the dining table. "Cup of tea?"

"Yes, that would be nice. Only, I can't be too long. Karen's expecting me back." The words stung Gary. After all this time he still wasn't used to the idea.

"I've bought some lovely home-made

biscuits," Gary's mum said, placing a tin on the table. "Help yourself." They sat at the table for some time, Bernadette, Eugene and Gary, eating the biscuits. It was like things used to be. Bernadette wanted to know all about the football match and Gary recalled almost every move, corner, free kick and goal. Then the phone rang. It was Karen. The spell had been broken, the dream ended. Gary had woken up.

"I'll have to go," Eugene said.

"Before you go, love, I was wondering if you and Karen would like to come for a meal? I was thinking about doing a . . . supper." Eugene's mouth fell open.

"What? You want me and Karen to come for a— It's not some sort of trick is it?"

"Don't be so suspicious! No, I've made a nice new friend and I wanted you meet him and his daughter."

"A new friend?" Eugene asked.

"Well, sort of. Anyways, would you like to come for supper?"

Eugene McNab was not the only one who was amazed by this invitation. Gary was stunned into silence and his dad said, "I'm sure Karen would be delighted."

"Great!" Bernadette said, brightly. "I'll phone you with the details."

Gary couldn't believe that his parents could

talk for so long without once mentioning the wedding.

Later that evening, Bernadette spread her paperwork all over the dining table, leaving Gary to watch television.

"Mum," he asked, as she frantically filled in forms. "What's a 'supper'? It's not just milk and biscuits, is it?"

She looked up, took her glasses off and gazed into the kitchen. "No! Ooh, it will be a lovely evening, Gary. Would you like to invite Robert?"

"But who are you inviting? It's not Matt Rossi is it?"

"Yes!" she said, amazement raising the tone of her voice. "How did you guess?"

"I remember you talking about him. You hardly know him, Mum. Are you inviting anyone else you met in the Castle Gardens.?"

"Don't be daft! We have met a few times for lunch, Gary."

"But why is he coming to supper?" Gary asked. He didn't feel happy about this. He didn't really want Matt Rossi in his house at all. Or, for that matter, Karen.

"Well, to be honest, Gary, between ourselves, I just wanted to show your dad and Karen."

"Show them what?" Gary asked, puzzled.

"That we can survive – that we can manage without him – and do very well! I felt so . . . hurt when that wedding invitation came. I just wanted to do something to show I'm getting on with my life, too."

Gary had the strangest feeling. It was a sort of panic. He wanted his mum to meet someone else, and yet . . . now it felt so uncomfortable.

This was not how he wanted it to be. Things were happening far too quickly.

SEVENTEEN

The supper was arranged for May Day bank holiday. Gary had been out all day with Robert, dreading the evening as if it was a visit to the dentist. When he returned home, his mum was in a terrible state.

"Everything's gone wrong, Gary!" Bernadette cried.

"What?" Gary asked, surveying the chaos in the kitchen.

"I've burnt the new potatoes, I put chilli powder instead of gravy powder in the casserole, and then I forgot to take the plastic off the broccoli before I put it on the stove!"

"Don't worry, Mum," Gary said as he stroked the back of his mother's hand. The kitchen looked really dreadful.

"What am I going to do, Gary. This is a major disaster!"

"It'll be all right, Mum."

"Gary, are you listening?" Bernadette said, in a panic. "I've ruined everything!"

"I've got an idea, Mum," Gary said. "Why don't we ring Gino's takeaway service?"

Bernadette recovered almost immediately. "What a brainwave! You are such a lovely, brilliant boy. Come on, let's get ordering."

Gino delivered the food before everyone arrived. Nothing else went to plan.

First of all, Francesca spilled orange juice over Bernadette's best lounge chair. "Francesca!" Matt Rossi scolded. "You're not normally so clumsy. Whatever is the matter?" Bernadette was furious but she kept smiling because she wanted everyone to enjoy themselves.

Then Karen started smoking.

"I'd rather you didn't smoke in the house, Karen," Bernadette said, curtly. Karen just glared at her. She didn't even look for an ash tray. At first she flicked the ash on to the carpet and then she used a *Souvenir of Colwyn Bay* to stub out her cigarette.

Nobody seemed to be saying much over supper. Gary's mum was too nervous and his dad seemed to be uncomfortable.

Karen left the table after each course to light up at the back door. Matt Rossi did the same.

"Just like being back at school, isn't it,

Matt?" Karen said in a loud voice so that everyone could hear. "Smoker's corner, where the grown-ups can't see us!"

From the back door there came the sound of giggling. Something was amusing them. Gary could see that this really upset his mum. "I didn't realise Karen smoked," Bernadette said before the pudding was served.

"Yes, she still does for some reason when she's feeling nervous," Eugene said. "Food's great, Bernadette. Your cooking has really improved," he added, trying to raise her spirits.

Bernadette was about to say who had cooked the meal when she spotted Francesca hanging on to every word. "Aren't you going to eat something, Francesca?" Bernadette asked.

"No, I'm not, it's too fatty. I'm not allowed to eat fat!" Francesca replied.

"Like you, you brat!" Gary hissed. Bernadette flashed a silencing look at her son.

When the dessert was served, Robert tried to make things better. "This is a brilliant pudding, Mrs McNab. It's really ace," he said between mouthfuls.

"Yes, it's great, Mum," Gary said trying to cover the awkward silence.

"Gary, why don't you show Francesca and Robert your new computer game while we have coffee?" Bernadette suggested.

Gary looked in amazement at his mother. He wanted desperately to protest but before he could say anything, Francesca ran out of the room and up the stairs.

"Pathetic computer!" Francesca announced as she sat at Gary's desk. "Got any good, non-football games?" she asked.

"No!" Robert shouted.

"Typical boys – all football and no brains!" Francesca said.

Robert and Gary laughed in a sneering way at Francesca even though Gary felt as if he'd been invaded. "You can't play with that game, it's brand new," Gary said hesitantly.

"What is it?" Francesca asked. "*Football Managers*? That's for four-year-olds!"

"Well, you'll be just about able to play it then," Robert sneered.

Francesca glared at Robert as her fingers danced over the keys.

"Leave it, please!" Gary said.

"What happens if I press this?" Francesca asked, as she pressed it. The logo disappeared from the scene. She giggled.

"That's it! I'm switching it off. You've ruined my brand new game!" Gary shouted. He and Robert dived towards the computer, desperate to prise Francesca away.

"I'm not staying here," Francesca said.

"Your computer's stupid, you're stupid, and this evening is boring, boring . . ." With that Francesca ran out of the room and down the stairs. A few minutes later, she announced that she wanted to go home. "I feel really, really sick, Dad."

"So sorry, Bernadette," Matt Rossi kept apologising as he backed out of the house. "I'll be in touch sometime next week. We'll meet up again, for lunch, maybe?"

"We'd better be going too, Eugene," Karen said firmly. "I've arranged to meet my sister in the morning to look at wedding dresses. Remember?"

"Oh, yes," Eugene said, distractedly.

"Thanks for coming," Bernadette said, weakly.

They left behind them a huge pile of dirty dishes and half the delicious pudding. Bernadette said she was going to bed. "I can't face the washing-up tonight," she said as she left the room without looking at Gary or Robert.

"Let's wash the plates," Robert suggested.

"Are you sure?" Gary said.

"And then finish that pudding!"

"I hate Karen," Gary said as he scrubbed a plate. "And Matt Rossi's not much better."

"You're right, Gary. We'll have to think of

something else for your mum. We can't let your mum go on seeing Matt Rossi – not with that stupid Francesca!"

EIGHTEEN

"If only I could cook, Gary. Things might be so different," Bernadette said with a huge sigh. She'd been saying this at some point every day since the meal. She sat on the chair, her legs tucked under her, browsing through a huge cookery book.

Gary was watching a football match. "What?" he said, suddenly becoming aware of his mum's words. He was alarmed to see that she looked so miserable. "What's up?"

"That meal. It was such a disaster," Gary's mum said as she cried quietly.

"No it wasn't, Mum. It was all right. That Francesca tried to spoil it, but that's because she's horrible and that's not your fault." Gary tried to console his mum in just the same way as she tried to comfort him when things went wrong.

"And Karen, she wasn't exactly the life and

soul of the party, was she?"

"No. Why did Dad have to bring her anyway?" Gary said.

Bernadette smiled. "Do you know, Gary, I think if I could cook, things would be so different. Look at Robert's gran, she's always making those lovely cakes and raising everyone's spirits. You love going to Robert's house, don't you?"

"Yes," Gary said, slightly bemused.

"And why? Because Robert's gran makes brilliant cakes!" Bernadette said. She was beginning to look happy again. "Don't worry, I'll be all right. It was nice having lunch with Matt Rossi but I think he's only looking for a mother for his little Francesca. No! I'd rather stick to my job and doing more with my little boy."

Gary felt relieved about Matt Rossi although a bit worried at the thought of having to spend more time with his mum. It was time for another shortlist.

The football match had finished and the commentator was interviewing the *Man of the Match*.

"Who's he?" Bernadette asked, distracted by the bright, smiling face of a City footballer.

"That's Tyrone Bradley, he's won the *Man of the Match*."

"Isn't he lovely," Mum said, her mood suddenly changing. "Such a kind, pleasant face."

It was taking a long time but Tyrone Bradley was, at long last, beginning to knock the ball around and get it in the back of the net.

On Monday morning, everyone who was anyone was talking about Tyrone's achievements for City:

"At the end of the day," Mr Doyle said, speaking like a true football commentator, "the lad's only human and he's got to get used to his new team mates."

"I was over the moon when he scored City's second," Danny Shah said.

"He couldn't do anything wrong," Kieran Sackville said.

"It's about time he did something with those million dollar legs," Ronan pronounced. "We're the ones paying his wages – us mugs!" (It was the most Gary had ever heard him say.)

"It was a classic goal, the first of many, we hope, son," Eugene said.

"Arrah, the lad needs to settle down, and nothing settles a young man like a wife and a couple of kids. I heard he was spending far too much time in those . . . nightclubs!" Robert's gran said.

"My mum thinks he's gorgeous. She's started

watching *Match of the Day* now, in case he's on," Robert said.

Gary had thought about this for a few days, now he was sure. "I think we should put him on top of our shortlist!"

NINETEEN

"Tyrone Bradley?" Robert shouted. "Everyone fancies Tyrone Bradley. He's got more girlfriends than team mates. Some of them are famous!"

Robert and Gary were doing Cookery. This week they were learning how to make shortcake. Gary thought he'd show his mum.

Robert's hands were covered in the flour and butter he was supposed to be rubbing together. As he spoke, he leaned them on the edge of the bowl. "Your mum wouldn't stand a chance with Tyrone Bradley."

"Why not?" Gary asked. He was annoyed at Robert dismissing *his* idea, and his mum. He scratched the side of his nose, leaving a great blob of the mixture on one cheek. When he tried to rub it off, some more of the mixture got into his hair. He was becoming even more annoyed.

"Well, she's not exactly like a model, is she? I

mean, Tyrone Bradley goes out with models and actresses and hairdressers."

"My mum's as good as any of them!"

"Gary McNab!" Mr Doyle snapped. "What are you playing at? You're covered in flour and butter. I hope you're not messing about."

"Sorry, Sir. I sneezed and then my nose was itchy," Gary said.

"What would your mother say if she could see the state you're in?"

"She probably wouldn't notice," Gary replied honestly. His mum often got into a mess in the kitchen.

"Maybe he wants to see your mum again!" Robert whispered. "That's why he mentioned her."

Gary hit him playfully on the back, leaving a palm print of uncooked shortcake. "Oops, sorry," Gary laughed nervously as he noticed the mess on Robert's jumper. Robert was wriggling about trying to see what the back of his jumper looked like.

As soon as the trays of shortcake were in the oven, the two boys were told to stand in the corridor. There they discussed the latest plan. "I'm going to write Tyrone Bradley a letter," Gary announced.

"What for?" Robert asked.

"To ask him if he'll meet my mum at the

football ground."

"You're daft."

"And d'you know what? I'm not going to keep it a secret this time. I'm going to tell her." The look on Robert's face suggested that he didn't think it such a good idea.

32 Wednesbury Road
Leicester

Dear Tyrone Bradley,
My mum, Bernadette, is a great fan of yours. She doesn't really like football but she thinks that you are great. She would like to meet you one Saturday after the match. I hope you don't mind me writing to you. My mum would write herself but she is very busy with her job. She's not a model but it's something like that. It would make her day if she could meet you.

Yours sincerely,
Gary McNab

108

THE TYRONE BRADLEY FAN CLUB
CITY FOOTBALL PROMOTIONS
CITY FOOTBALL GROUND

How ya doin' Gary!

Thanks for the letter. Welcome to the fan club! Tyrone receives over 500 letters a week. Everybody loves him! Who wouldn't?

Tyrone isn't able to meet your mum right now but he will be in your area soon.

Would you like to join our club? Here's a form and a money-off voucher for Tyrone's new video: Fun Football, the Tyrone Bradley Way.

Do you want to sign our petition? We want the City council to rename the Victoria underpass, the TYRONE BRADLEY SUBWAY. Every name counts!

Join our club and you'll find out lots more.

Byeeee!
Georgie Malpass

TWENTY

Gary had thought it would be so easy. He would write to Tyrone Bradley and Tyrone would write back saying he wanted to meet Gary's mum. He hadn't realised that Tyrone Bradley was so famous that he had his own fan club.

Well, Tyrone Bradley might be famous but *his* mum was important. He imagined the story on the front page of the *Mercury*:

SOCCER SUPERSTAR AND LEADING MIDWIFE WED

The more Gary thought about it, the more he realised that Tyrone Bradley was the man for his mum. He even began to see her new signature: *Bernadette Bradley*. And when City won the cup, he'd be on the open-top bus in the victory parade with his mum and Tyrone.

They might even film *Football Focus* at his house – Tyrone in his designer sportswear, gently kicking the ball to Gary while talking about his hopes for City to win the League.

But, how could they get to meet Tyrone Bradley?

Mr Doyle wasn't much help. "Tyrone Bradley? What do you want to meet him for?" he asked as he pinned up a new display. Quite often Gary and Robert came into the classroom before school to talk about football.

"Well, he's brilliant," Robert said.

"That's a matter of opinion. I think he's a fly-by-night myself. Even though he has a three year contract, I reckon he'll be off next season. Now if, on the other hand, you wanted to meet Stephan Kanchinski. . ."

"No thanks, Sir," Gary said, quickly dismissing the idea.

"He could teach you a thing or two about goalkeeping," Mr Doyle said.

Gary wanted to say that his mum wasn't at all interested in goalkeeping but he decided it was best to say nothing.

Time was moving on, it was almost the end of May. Soon, Dad and Karen would be married and Gary's mum might, in desperation, choose any old person for a husband. Something had to be done.

Gary asked Robert's gran what she would do if she really, really wanted to meet someone famous.

"Like who?" she asked.

"Like the pope!" Robert said, as if struck by a brainwave. He thought that the pope was his gran's Tyrone Bradley.

"Well, I'll tell you this much. You might not know her but there's a woman who lives up beyond the park, Mrs Igoe. Your mother will know her, Gary. I heard that when she went to Rome, she told the officials in St Peter's Square she was very ill so that she could go up near the front."

"And what happened?" Gary asked, slightly shocked.

"She met him all right. She shook his hand and apparently he said that he hoped she'd be better soon!"

"Would you do that, Gran?" Robert asked.

"I would not! Well, not for the pope, anyway. It might be different if it was Des O'Connor or Daniel O'Donnell."

"Who?" Gary and Robert asked together. Robert's gran looked up to the ceiling and carried on with her baking.

Later on, when Robert's gran was safely out

of earshot, Gary and Robert discussed tactics. "That's given me an idea,' Robert said.

"What has?"

"What Gran was saying about the pope. I've had an idea about your mum and Tyrone Bradley. I know how they could meet."

Gary listened carefully to Robert's latest idea.

"No! I'm not doing that. Mum would kill me!" Gary protested.

"It's the only way."

TWENTY-ONE

"I'm not going to say my mum's very ill just so that she can meet a City footballer. No way!" said Gary. "Anyway, Tyrone Bradley won't be interested in marrying her if she's ill."

"She can have a miraculous recovery. Go on, Gary."

"No! For a start off, it's a lie. You shouldn't lie about things like that. Secondly, if my mum found out she'd kill me."

"She won't find out," Robert pleaded.

"Go on, Gary. Let's try it anyways," Robert said.

"No!" Gary shouted. "My mum would do her nut."

"Here, I've got some good notepaper," Robert said, helpfully. "Let's start writing, Gary. We'll think of something."

32 Wednesbury Road
Leicester

Dear Mr Tyrone Bradley,

My mother, Bernadette, is suffering from a mystery illness. The doctors just don't know what is wrong with her. Even though she is very unhappy with this illness she still follows the City. She is always really happy when the City wins. Me and my friend, Robert, were thinking that it would be a great surprise for my mum if she could meet you. We both think you are great.

Please write and let us know when we could all meet up with you.

Yours sincerely,

Gary McNab

P.S. My mum gets quite upset about her illness so it's probably best if you don't mention it when we meet.

"Shall I post it on the way home?" Gary asked.
"No, leave it with me, Gary. I'll just neaten it up a bit and then send it off," Robert said, helpfully. "We should get a reply quite soon."

Robert was right. Within a few days they had received a positive reply.
"The tickets are here!" Robert announced as

he cycled into Gary's front garden. "Well, not exactly the tickets. We have to pick them up from Reception after our—"

"Shush! Don't let my mum hear," Gary whispered. "She's just in the hall."

"What are you two up to?" Gary's mum asked as he and Robert crept quietly in the back door.

"We've had some good news, Mum," Gary announced. His mum raised a questioning eyebrow. "Robert's been given some free tickets for City's next mid-week home match."

"Great!" mum said.

"The only thing is, Mum," Gary said, "we have to have an adult with us."

"Do you? Well, I suppose that's a good thing. You'd better get in touch with your dad then, give him plenty of notice," Bernadette said as she walked from room to room, checking the windows were locked.

"No!" Gary shouted. His mum looked quite surprised. "He's too busy. Couldn't you come with us, for a change?"

"What about your mum, Robert? Or your gran?"

"No, Mrs McNab. I've already asked them. They don't want to go."

"Oh, go on, Mum. We can't go to the match unless we have an adult with us," Gary pleaded.

"Just let me check my diary, then I'll have to

go to work. What date did you say it was?"

"A week on Tuesday," Robert said hopefully.

"Oh no!" Bernadette said, laughing. "I'm on call that evening. That means I can go with you but I'll have to wear my uniform and take my bleep!"

"What?" Gary said, unable to believe his ears. "Can't you wear something nice for a change?"

"Oh, Gary!" Bernadette said in a mocking tone. Then, after a final check of the contents of her briefcase, she opened the front door. "Now Gary, be good today," With that she walked smartly out to her car, touching her chest watch and pocket pens as she did so, checking that all was well.

"Do you want to see the letter from the manager?" Robert asked in a distracted manner. He held it out for Gary.

With the Compliments of the City Football Club

Dear Robert and Gary,

Here's your invitation. We look forward to seeing you at City's next evening home game. If you need wheelchair access for your mother, let us know beforehand. Hopefully, she will be well enough to attend. Tyrone will help out with your mum's wheelchair if necessary.

We ask you to report to Reception at 5 p.m. on the day.

Regards,

Neil Warren
Publicity and Promotions

"What's this about a wheelchair, Robert?"

"After you left the other day I added a bit to the letter. I was worried. I thought it would be better if I said that . . . Well, we might not have got the tickets."

"So what *did* you write?" Gary asked, cautiously.

"I said your mum was so poorly that sometimes she had to use a wheelchair."

"You didn't!"

"I did. I didn't think we'd get to meet Tyrone Bradley if she was just a little bit ill."

"I don't think that you should have done that. What about all the people who really are in wheelchairs and want to meet Tyrone Bradley?"

Robert hadn't thought of that. He felt awful for a bit.

"Oh no!" Gary sighed. "Not only is she perfectly healthy, she'll be wearing her uniform and carrying that briefcase.

"Still, at least she'll get to meet Tyrone Bradley." Robert said in a comforting voice. "And that's all that matters!"

TWENTY-TWO

They walked to the match. Bernadette swung her big, black briefcase as if she was a vet going to deliver calves at a remote farm. Gary and Robert walked slightly in front of her.

"They might think she's a doctor," Robert whispered.

"Don't be daft," Gary said.

They arrived at the ground just before five o'clock. Mr Warren was waiting to greet them. "You're most welcome, Mrs McNab," he shook Bernadette's hand firmly. "You are very courageous," he almost whispered this last sentence.

"I am courageous, coming to the match with this pair, you're not kidding," Bernadette said, laughing.

"Now then," Neil Warren said, rubbing his hands together. "First of all I'll take you

119

to the VIP lounge for a drink. Would you like to follow me?"

Neil Warren began to run quickly up the stairs and then, as if remembering himself, he slowed down. "I'm sorry, Mrs McNab, can you manage these stairs all right?"

"Yes," Bernadette said, hesitantly.

"Only we can . . . get some help if you need it," Neil Warren said, through the side of his mouth. "We always try to help our . . . people from the local community."

"Yes, I can see. It's very kind of you," Bernadette said. She was a little surprised at his attitude.

"Now, what have you got in that briefcase? All your dressings and tablets and so on?" Mr Warren asked. Gary noticed that he spoke to his mum as if she was deaf.

"Not exactly," Bernadette said.

In the VIP lounge, Neil Warren showed them to a table. "Tyrone will be joining you a little later," He said. "Now, Mrs McNab, if there are any emergencies, ask the bar for assistance. They can phone out and summon help."

"It's all right, Mr Warren, I've got my bleep."

"Your bleep?" Mr Warren questioned. His face was a picture of confusion. He backed away from the three of them and with, "I'll see you later," he rushed off.

Tyrone Bradley eventually arrived at the table as they were finishing their drinks. "Hi, I'm Tyrone. You must be Mrs McNab."

Gary and Robert were so stunned at being in such close proximity to their hero that their mouths fell open.

"In a moment, I'll take you down to the dressing room and then on to the pitch where you'll receive your souvenir football."

"That's extremely kind of you, Tyrone," Bernadette said. Gary couldn't believe how relaxed she was. In fact, she spoke to Tyrone as if he was one of Gary's friends rather than a prospective boyfriend.

"Do you think you'll be able to manage the stairs, Bernadette? Don't mind if I call you Bernadette, do you?" Tyrone asked.

"Call me anything you like, Tyrone," Gary's mum said, laughing.

"Well, will you . . . will you be able to manage the stairs, Bernie? There is a lift if you need to put your . . . but you don't have one do you?"

Gary and Robert were beginning to sweat. Bernadette looked pleasantly puzzled.

Tyrone Bradley walked down the stairs holding Bernadette's elbow as if she were an elderly aunt.

"I can manage," she said, half laughing.

"The thing is, with these steps you think you can manage. Have you got your tablets and dressings and that in your briefcase?"

"Are you playing today, Tyrone?" Gary asked quickly before his mum could reveal the contents of her briefcase.

:"Yes," Tyrone snapped. Then, in a gentler tone, "What's this uniform you're wearing, Bernie?"

"I'm a midwife, Tyrone," she said.

"Will you autograph our—" Robert said, trying to steer the conversation away from Bernadette's uniform.

"Are you still working even though you're—" Tyrone said.

"Yes, but my bleep will reach this far," she replied.

"Oh, great," Tyrone said, totally confused by her attitude. "Are you waiting for a transplant or something?" he asked. Bernadette smiled at him. She thought he was joking.

On the pitch, a few minutes later, Bernadette stood between Tyrone Bradley and Neil Warren. She put her arm around

Tyrone's shoulder before the photo was taken. "At least your mum seems to like Tyrone," Robert whispered.

Bernadette was presented with a football and a pennant. Tyrone whispered something as he placed the gifts in her arms.

"That's it, that's it!" Robert hissed. "He's probably asked her out."

"What did he say, Mum?" Gary asked as they took their seats for the match. "What was Tyrone Bradley whispering about?"

"He said he hopes I'll be feeling much better soon. Do I look peaky?"

"There's Timmy Stevens" Robert shouted, spotting someone from their class. "Hey, up, Timmy!" He shouted.

"And Kieran Sackville!" Gary joined in. "Sackville!" he shouted.

As they searched through the crowd looking for familiar faces, Robert suddenly spotted something strange.

"Hey, up, Gary. Look down there. Second row, three seats in."

"It's—" Gary spotted Matt Rossi and was about to shout his name so that his mum could look but he was silenced by a sharp elbow in the ribs.

"Have you seen who's with him?" Robert whispered.

"It's Karen," Gary said, amazed. "That's weird."

"Karen with Matt Rossi," Robert said, quietly giggling. "I wonder if your dad knows?"

Five minutes before the final whistle, Bernadette's bleep went off. "I'll see you back home, lads," she said, forcing the match programme into her briefcase. "I'd better not hang around in case it's an emergency."

Then to the amazement of Neil Warren, she skipped down the steps leading to the main reception area. "Thanks a million," she said. "I can't wait to see myself in the paper!" She nudged Neil's shoulder in a playful way as she passed him.

"Neither can I," he replied in a surprised tone.

She didn't see Tyrone Bradley missing an open goal. Neither did she see the press release that the City Football Club had given to the *Mercury*.

As they walked home, discussing Tyrone Bradley's terrible miss, Robert and Gary were blissfully unaware of the story that would be splashed across the following evening's *Mercury*. As far as they were concerned, it had been a great success.

Bernadette had met Tyrone and they had liked one another. True happiness and free City tickets for evermore.

TWENTY-THREE

Gary couldn't concentrate at school the next day. He kept thinking about what it would be like when Tyrone came to visit. He'd probably use his four-wheel drive Range Rover (Gary had seen it on *Football Focus*) to take his mum out to the pictures or, possibly, to Gino's. No, she wouldn't go to Gino's. That was where they went with Dad. No, they wouldn't go there.

At times he might find it boring when people asked, "Will you get Tyrone to sign this?" They might have to move to a bigger house with a long, gravel drive. Tyrone would need plenty of space to turn his car.

Mr Doyle spotted Gary day-dreaming. "Are you stuck, Double?" he asked, crouching beside Gary's desk.

"When does the *Mercury* come out?" Gary said, without thinking.

"Gary McNab, sometimes you are not on the

same planet as the rest of us." Mr Doyle spoke softly, amused by Gary's questions. "Why do you ask?"

"Me and Robert will be in it tonight!" Gary announced. "We were at the match last night. We saw Tyrone Bradley."

"So did nineteen thousand other fans, Gary!" Mr Doyle said.

"No, Sir. We actually met him. Me and Robert. We talked to him like I'm talking to you. He was this far away." Gary stretched his arm out to show Mr Doyle how close he'd been to his hero.

"Did you indeed. How did you manage that?"

Robert giggled. "It took a lot of planning, Sir."

"Well, good for you, lads." Then, as he stood up, Mr Doyle said, "I look forward to seeing tonight's *Mercury*."

"So do we!" Gary and Robert said together.

CITY'S CONQUEST HELPS BRAVE MUM'S BATTLE

Brave mum, Mrs Bernadette McNab, took her battle against a mystery illness to City's final match of the season last night. "I've had a wonderful time," she said after meeting City's million pound signing, Tyrone Bradley.

Wheelchair

Neil Warren, City's Publicity and Promotions Manager, said, "This is one of the bravest women I've met in a long time. Bernadette was smiling and happy all evening, despite having a mystery illness which sometimes confines her to a wheelchair."

Sons

Mrs McNab's condition came to the attention of the City Football Club when her sons, Gary and Robert, wrote to ask if she could meet Tyrone Bradley. "We get hundreds of letters like this every week but this one really touched my heart," Mr Warren said. "Mrs McNab is lucky to have such supportive and caring boys as Gary and Robert."

Our picture shows the McNab family with Tyrone Bradley and Neil Warren.

Would you like to meet your favourite City player?
Details on page 17.

Gary and Robert were stunned. They stood outside the newsagent staring at the local paper in disbelief.

"They didn't have to say that," Gary said.

"What will your mum say?" Robert said, not really expecting an answer. Cars and lorries rushed past on the busy road. Life went on.

"We can't let her see it," Gary replied, dazed. "She never buys the paper. We've got to keep quiet about it."

"Well, I suppose that's all right then, I hope," Robert said, trying to reassure himself as well as Gary.

It was true, Bernadette never bought the *Mercury*. Even when Gary's school choir was photographed winning a prize at the Music Festival. So she didn't see the story or the picture. She didn't know anything about it.

Until seven o'clock. That's when the phone calls began – and the trouble.

"Gary!"

The woman who lived three doors away had given her a copy. "You look lovely in the photograph," she said brightly. "I had no idea. I hope you'll be feeling much, much better soon."

"Gary!" She had to shout several times before he appeared at the top of the stairs. She was too furious to walk up. Shouting made her feel slightly better.

"What's up, Mum?" Gary asked, all innocently.

"What is this? Have you seen it? Come down and explain what's going on! *Now*!"

Gary's heart fell as he noticed the dreaded newspaper in his mother's hand. What could he say?

"You have got some explaining to do and I am *waiting*!"

TWENTY-FOUR

Everyone in the world had read the *Mercury*. Everyone! Even though it was only a local paper. Eugene McNab had read it and rang up to see what was going on.

Robert's mum, Ronan and Robert's gran had read it. Mr Doyle had read it. He bought the paper specially but he didn't say anything. He waited to see what Trouble and Double would get up to next.

"What do you think your mum will do?" Robert asked. He felt so miserable about the way things had turned out.

"I wish we'd never heard of Tyrone Bradley. I wish City had never signed him!" Gary said.

"But what will she do?" Robert asked again.

"I don't know. I'll try and find out."

"You won't do anything, will you Mum?" Gary asked. "I won't do it again. We were only doing it for your own good."

"Really! But why were you doing it?" Bernadette asked. She was furious. In fact she had been furious for over a week.

"I've told you, Mum. Me and Robert thought you'd like to meet Tyrone Bradley. You said you liked him."

"By why did you say I had a mystery illness and sometimes needed a wheelchair?" She didn't look at Gary as she attacked the far corners at the back of one of the kitchen cupboards.

"I keep telling you, Mum. It's hard to meet him if you're normal. We tried."

"Gary, I can't understand why you should lie about such a thing. It is so wrong to lie and to . . . make light of other people's disabilities. Don't you understand that?"

"Yes, Mum, but—"

"There are no excuses for doing something like that. None whatsoever! And why did you want me to meet him anyway?"

Gary had never seen his mum so angry.

"Why?" his mum asked again.

"I'm sorry, Mum," Gary said, quietly. "Honestly, I'm sorry."

"What?" Bernadette said, taken aback.

"I'm sorry. Me and Robert shouldn't have done it. I didn't want to upset you."

Bernadette sat down at the dining table, her anger melting as she sighed. "Why did you do it, love? Just answer me that?"

"We did it because—"

"Did you and Robert want to meet Tyrone and you thought it might be easier if you made them think you had a disabled mother? Was that it?"

"Something like that, Mum."

Bernadette rested her head on one hand and closed her eyes. Gary couldn't help wishing none of it had happened. Tyrone Bradley had made his mum so miserable.

"I want you to promise me something, Gary. Promise me you'll never, ever, do anything like this again. Never!"

"I promise, Mum," and he meant it.

Bernadette ruffled his hair. "Good lad. I won't do anything else, Gary, because I think you've punished yourself enough with all the misery it's brought. Now, you will keep your promise won't you?"

"Yes, Mum. Can I call for Robert now?"

"No. I think it's best if you have a little break from playing with Robert." With that, Gary's Mum returned to her work in the kitchen.

Gary sat, slumped across the sofa, gazing up at the light in the centre of the room. He counted each plaster ring around the lampshade. What a waste of time, he thought.

The door bell rang. Gary sat up quickly,

hoping it would be Robert.

"Get that, will you, Gary?"

It wasn't Robert. It was Gary's dad. He was unshaven and looked tired as he leaned against the porch door.

"What's up?" Gary asked, forgetting to say hello. "It's not my Saturday with you, is it?"

"Who is it?" Bernadette called from the kitchen.

"It's me," Eugene said, sounding thoroughly fed up. "Can I come in?"

Bernadette came to the front door. "Is everything all right? It's not your Saturday, is it?"

"No." Eugene walked slowly and uncertainly into the hall. "I was wondering . . . could I stay here for a few days?"

TWENTY-FIVE

"Brilliant! Brilliant, Dad!" Gary pulled at his dad's sleeve. He wanted to climb up on to his shoulders and hug him properly. What a day! Suddenly, just like that, the whole world had changed. Dad was coming back to stay and everything, *everything* would be all right. They could forget all about Tyrone Bradley, Matt Rossi, Tamsin, and Karen. Mum and Dad would probably want to have a good chat, catch up with things so, Gary hoped, he'd be able to call for Robert.

Gary tried to pull his dad along the hall. He wanted to shout, "Hug him, Mum. Don't let him go again."

"I don't understand," Bernadette said, "What's happened?"

"Oh, it's a long story," Gary's dad said, wearily.

"What about Karen?" Bernadette asked. Gary had wanted to ask the same question but he didn't want to spoil the moment.

Bernadette shut the door quietly behind Eugene. The three of them stood in the hall. "Well?" she asked.

"Well, what?"

"You're supposed to be getting married again the week after next. What's happened?"

"Dad, do you fancy watching a bit of the cricket?" Gary asked.

"Gary, be quiet for a minute," Bernadette said gently. "Tell you what. Would you put the kettle on for me and your dad?"

From the kitchen he could barely hear their hushed voices. "Karen wants me out of the flat," his dad said.

Gary pressed his ear to the door. What are they saying? He could hear the low murmur of conversation but he couldn't make out their words.

"If only Robert was here," Gary said as he paced around the kitchen. "He'd think of a way of listening. I'll ring him." Gary opened the kitchen door. "Mum, sorry to disturb you," he shouted, "but can I ring Robert?"

There was no reply. They didn't even seem to be talking anymore. Then, suddenly, Dad opened the lounge door. "Has the kettle boiled yet, Gary?" he called.

Bernadette came out to make the tea. She moved briskly about the kitchen. "I bet you're dying to know what's going on," she said, almost mischievously.

"Sort of."

"Well, you might find this hard to believe . . ."

Gary did find it very hard to believe. Karen had asked Dad to leave. She had met someone else. She had found somebody whose child adored her, and little Francesca was—

"Francesca?" Gary asked. "Not Francesca—" his face revealed that he knew exactly which Francesca his mother was talking about.

"Yes! How did you know?" Bernadette said, surprised.

Gary shrugged his shoulders nervously. "Dunno really. I just guessed."

Gary's mind raced. What if Matt Rossi told Karen about how he had met his mum? They would probably laugh about his mum. He hated Karen more than ever.

Then, through the awkward silence, the doorbell rang again. Gary ran to open it.

TWENTY-SIX

Gary couldn't speak. He tried but his mouth and his throat weren't working. He held the door back, unable to believe his eyes. Tyrone Bradley, soccer superstar, and City's million pound signing stood on his front doorstep with a huge bouquet.

Tyrone Bradley was wearing a professional smile that began to fade slightly at the edges when it wasn't returned by Bernadette.

"What do you want?" she asked.

"What a lovely surprise!" Eugene said, trying to cover for Bernadette's coolness.

"Hi!" Tyrone Bradley said, cheerfully. "Some flowers for you, Bernie. Just wanted to say sorry."

"For what?" she asked. "And don't call me Bernie."

"For getting the story wrong and

embarrassing you with the thing in the *Mercury*." Tyrone's smile had disappeared.

"Thanks," she relieved Tyrone of the bouquet.

Then, as if from nowhere, another man appeared. "Hang on, hang on," he said. "Let me introduce myself. My name is Duane Denver. I'm Tyrone's manager. I've brought a photographer with me. I thought we could take a quick snap, send it down to the *Mercury*, show all is forgiven." He laughed nervously. "The lad could do with a bit of good publicity."

"Are you serious?" Bernadette asked incredulously.

This wasn't quite what Duane had imagined her response would be. A photographer stepped up beside him.

"Now, if you stand out here, Mrs McNab, we can have one of you accepting the flowers from Tyrone."

"It's really lovely of you," Eugene said. "But this isn't actually a good time."

"I don't want my photo in the paper," Bernadette said confidently, and thrust the flowers back at Tyrone.

"Oh, come on, Bernie," Tyrone Bradley said, trying to coax her. He waved the bouquet at her.

"No! You'd better go now. I accept your apology but you're not going to get any free publicity out of it."

"Mum," Gary whined. "This is Tyrone Bradley."

"There, you see! Your boy is speaking sense," Duane Denver said. As he tried to persuade Bernadette, the peach-coloured roses seemed to be wilting already. "Come on, it won't hurt and it'll only take a minute."

"No!" Bernadette said firmly. "I think it's best if you go."

"Mum," Gary pleaded again.

"Do you realise who this lad is?" Duane said. Tyrone couldn't manage even a hint of a smile now. "He is Tyrone Bradley, City's million pound signing! Nobody tells him where to go or what to do. He has been sent by the club to apologise and to make sure it reaches the front page of the local rag. Now, are you going to co-operate?"

"Yeah. Are you going to do as you're told?" Tyrone added.

Gary didn't like the way Tyrone Bradley was speaking to his mother. But Tyrone was Gary's hero. How do you tell your hero not to be rude?

There was another uncomfortable silence.

"Are you?" Tyrone repeated angrily.

"I don't think you should speak to my mum like that," Gary said, almost in a whisper. He couldn't believe himself.

"Are you telling me what to do, shrimp?" Tyrone Bradley hissed, surprised by Gary's words.

"I don't think you should speak to my mum like that," Gary said again, a bit louder this time.

"Duane, I've had enough of this. Come on," he tugged at Duane Denver's sleeve.

The two men rushed out of the McNab's front garden and piled into Tyrone's Range Rover, flinging the peach roses into the back as they did so.

Gary cycled over to Robert's. He couldn't wait to tell him all that had happened.

"You told Tyrone Bradley where to go?"

"Not exactly."

"I don't believe you," Robert said.

It was hard for Gary to work out what was real and what was in his head at that moment. He wasn't surprised when Robert doubted his story. "My dad's back as well," Gary told Robert.

"You're kidding!"

"About five minutes before Tyrone

Bradley called."

"Are you serious?"

"It's weird though."

"So that's it then," Robert said with some finality.

"What?"

"Your mum and dad. If they're back together again you don't need to look for anyone for your mum."

"No. He's not properly back. Mum says he's in between flats."

"Why? That seems a bit daft."

"Yeah. It's a bit strange."

"I thought you'd be glad your dad's back."

"Well . . . I am and I'm not. It seems like the house is too crowded. Me and my mum, we'd got used to being by ourselves. But then in another way it's good having Dad there for someone different to talk to . . ." Gary's voice trailed off.

"What about Karen?" Robert asked.

"She's run off with Matt Rossi."

"What? You are joking!"

"Worse than that." Gary said.

"What could be worse than that?" Robert asked innocently.

"If my mum finds out the truth about Matt Rossi, we're in dead trouble."

But it wasn't Dad or Karen or Matt Rossi who told Bernadette how she had met her 'perfect partner'.

She found out for herself.

TWENTY-SEVEN

Gary's hands shook that day at school. He looked pale and troubled. Even Mr Doyle noticed.

"What's up, Double?" he asked. "You're not coming down with something are you?"

Robert nudged him. "You all right?"

No, he wasn't all right. This was the worst day of his life. Well, the worst one since Karen had sat outside in the van, chewing gum and reading a magazine. Waiting for his dad.

First thing, Mum was annoyed anyway, because Dad was in the bathroom for ages.

Then there was a form. About football. "Have you signed my form, Mum?"

"What form?" Bernadette asked. She didn't want to be delayed any longer.

"Mr Doyle's doing another soccer skills course. You have to sign the form by today."

"No, Gary. I haven't seen the form. Must

be in your bag. Empty it out. Let me take a look." She was impatient to get to work.

Bernadette picked up every note and smoothed them quickly. Even the note from _Perfect Partners! The special cut-price offer._

"What is this? Where did you get it from?" Bernadette asked. At first she was smiling slightly. She was amused to think Gary had kept such an advertisement.

Then out of the weeks-ago depths of his bag, Bernadette found another note. It contained the name of her Perfect Partner. Matt Rossi.

"Gary McNab," she said, quietly but fiercely. "I want to talk to you."

That's when Gary's hand had started to shake. He watched his mum pace around the room. Then into the kitchen, the hall and up the stairs. She was biting her knuckles.

Gary felt sick and cold and hot and shaky. Enormous drums beat inside his ears. His forehead was wet with sweat, his mouth dry and still. He heard his mum asking his dad to wait a few minutes, so they could sort things out together.

"Wish I could but I can't," he protested. "Got to open the shop."

"Is this what I think it is?" Bernadette asked. Gary didn't need to answer.

"Was it for a laugh?" Bernadette asked.

"No."

"Or a dare?"

"No."

"Then why? What made my lovely boy do this?" His mother was clearly upset and shaken.

"Robert said—"

"Robert! Was he in on this? Why?"

"Well, when Dad said he was going to marry Karen, Robert said you'd probably meet somebody else so—"

"You thought you'd help me?"

"Yes."

"So you wrote to Perfect Partners?"

There was a long pause whilst Gary thought. "After we tried Mr Doyle," he said.

"What?" It was almost a scream. "What do you mean – Mr Doyle?"

"We thought . . . I'm sorry," Gary muttered.

"Why? Why did you do it?" Bernadette hissed.

"I said, I'm sorry, Mum."

"That isn't enough, Gary. I want to know exactly why you did it. Don't you realise how much you've let me down, Gary?"

At that moment, something inside Gary snapped. He was fed up with being told off when he'd only been trying to help . "Well, you and Dad let *me* down! Nobody asks me about anything!" he shouted, trying not to cry. Shaking, wanting to be hugged.

"What? What do you mean?"

"Dad didn't ask if I liked Karen or anything. I was worried, Mum. I was worried that you might come back with someone horrible – a man who would live in our house and—"

His mum slumped into a chair as his voice trailed off.

"So?"

"And if he didn't like me he'd say that I'd have to go and live with Dad and Karen and I HATE Karen! So me and Robert thought it would be best if we chose someone for you – just in case."

There was a long silence. Gary was still shaking but, in a way, relieved that it was all out in the open.

"I didn't realise, Gary. Why didn't you tell me how you felt."

"You're always busy, Mum – with babies and paperwork. We wanted you to meet someone nice, someone who liked the things that I like. Someone who'd get on with me. Someone like Dad."

"Searching for someone like Dad?"

Bernadette said. "Why? I thought we were doing fine by ourselves. I don't want anybody else right now."

"Not even Dad?" Gary asked, hopefully.

"Not even Dad, Gary."

TWENTY-EIGHT

Gary's mind was elsewhere all day. When Mr Doyle asked him, "What's up?" Robert had to nudge him again. "You all right?"

No, he wasn't. "Mum found them," he mumbled, more to himself than anyone.

"Found what?" Robert asked, intrigued.

"Yes. What did she find?" Mr Doyle asked, crouching beside Gary's desk, wanting to help.

"The letters," Gary whispered. "From Perfect Partners. About Matt Rossi."

"You're joking!" Robert said in amazement.

"What are you talking about?" Mr Doyle persisted.

Gary stared straight ahead. His mother's words boomed inside his head. You've let me down, you've let me down.

"I didn't mean to let her down," he said.

"What is he talking about, Robert" Mr Doyle asked.

While the rest of the class discussed their Technology projects, Robert told Mr Doyle all about Perfect Partners.

"But my mum found the letters and she's really, really upset," Gary said. "I don't know why. We were only trying to help."

Mr Doyle opened his mouth to speak several times. He looked as though he was searching carefully for the right words. "You can't make people do things, Gary," he said.

"What do you mean?" Gary asked.

"Well . . . you wanted your dad to stay at home but he felt he needed to move out. You couldn't make him stay. You wanted your mum to find a new man but she didn't want one. It's hard enough for grown-ups when they love someone and that someone doesn't love them back. Even when you're an adult, Gary, you can't always make what you want happen," Mr Doyle said.

"What do you mean, Sir?" Robert asked.

"How about I tell you a little secret?" Mr Doyle said, almost whispering. "I would absolutely love to be married and have children—"

"You'd make a good dad, Sir, if you don't

mind me saying," Robert interrupted.

"Thanks, Robert," Mr Doyle replied.

"Well . . . most of the time you would!" Robert added. Gary giggled, recovering a little.

"Anyway, as I was saying—" Mr Doyle continued. Robert was about to interrupt again but Mr Doyle held up his hand as if to silence the interruption. "The thing is, no matter how much I'd like to be married and have children, I have to find the *right* person. Nobody else can make it happen for me. Do you see what I mean, Gary?"

"I think so, Sir."

"And, meanwhile, I make the very best of life." Mr Doyle said.

"Even though you're a teacher, Sir?" Robert interrupted again.

"Yes, Robert," Mr Doyle said, smiling. "You just have to make the best of things. You *already* have a dad, Gary. He's always there for you. You don't have to hunt for another one. Remember that!" Mr Doyle ruffled Gary's hair. "Come on, Double and Trouble, pack your things away. It's almost time for the bell."

"Thanks Mr Doyle," Gary said, smiling at Robert.

* * *

They went straight to Robert's house after school. "I'll keep out of Mum's way for a bit longer," Gary said.

The kitchen was full of the smell of warm cake. Three of Gran's new creations sat on the cooling tray.

"How's the matchmaking going?" Robert's gran asked.

"Terrible!" Robert said. "She found out."

"Did she? Well, isn't that an awful thing? Still, never mind, matchmaking never was a smooth affair. You can always start again when the dust settles," Robert's gran said.

"Never again!" Gary declared.

"Fair enough," Robert's gran said. "Gary, you're looking a bit peaky today. Would you like to take a cake home for tea?"

"Thanks!" Gary said, delighted with her present.

"And maybe next time you're over, you can tell me exactly what went wrong with the old matchmaking," Robert's gran suggested.

Back home. Bernadette and Eugene were sitting at the table. The tea was made.

"Present from Robert's gran," Gary said, placing the warm lemon cake in the centre of the table. He wanted them to smile. He was fed up with long faces and miserable moods.

"I've said I'm sorry," he said.

Eugene cleared his throat. "Gary, what you did was very wrong."

"I know," Gary whispered.

"But it wasn't all your fault," Bernadette said.

"Robert's sorry, too," Gary said, looking up at his mum.

"No, no, we don't mean that," Eugene said.

"You were right, Gary. We didn't ask you what you wanted," Bernadette said, placing her hand over Gary's. "And we're sorry about that."

As he looked at his mum and dad, Gary wished for two things: for the lemon cake to last forever and . . . for his mum and dad to always sit there. Every morning, every evening.

"What are you thinking, Gary?" Bernadette asked, breaking into his thoughts.

"Oh, nothing much. I was just wondering if we could have some lemon cake? And . . . what's happening Dad? Are you stopping here or what?" Gary asked.

"Gary, you don't have to look for another dad," Eugene said, overlooking Gary's question. "I'm your dad. Whenever you need me, I'll be there for you. I'll always be your dad. Always!" And he pulled Gary to him and gave him a long hard hug.

"I know. Thanks Dad," Gary said, smiling.

TWENTY-NINE

The following evening Gary and Robert cycled to the park together. They chained their bikes to the bowling green bench in Eastern park before paying for the pitch and putt.

"It must be so weird," Robert said as they sat in the long grass waiting for their turn.

"It is," Gary agreed.

"Are they back together again or what?"

"Dad's back home," Gary said. "But he's leaving again as soon as he finds another place."

"Don't you want him to stay?" Robert asked, intrigued by the situation.

"Sort of. But, it might not be the right thing for him to stay. Well, that's what Mum and Dad say."

"Why don't we do something to make him stay?" Robert suggested.

"Like what?"

"Oh, I don't know."

"Anyway, we can't. Mum doesn't want him to stay," Gary said with some finality. "We can't make her do something she doesn't w—"

"Your mum didn't know she wanted to meet Mr Doyle or Matt Rossi, or Tyrone Bradley," Robert said, interrupting Gary.

"That's the point . . ." Gary said, almost thinking aloud. "Hey, Robert! Remember what Mr Doyle said when we were in the Brecon Beacons?"

Robert looked puzzled. "No."

"He said, 'If you can abseil down this cliff . . .'"

"'You can do anything!'" Robert finished the sentence for Gary.

"Sometimes you can, sometimes you can't . . . Or shouldn't!" said Gary.

"Well, I've got an idea," said Robert. "And it's a really good idea this time!"

"Oh, NO!" Gary groaned.